Dex had transferred to Hudson High from California the week after school started, and everything about him was West Coasty—his bronze suntan, his streaky yellow hair, his ocean-colored eyes. Every girl at Hudson looked at him with awe, so when he pulled up to the curb on his motorcycle that afternoon and suggested in a husky whisper, "Let me give you a lift, babe," it never occurred to Megan to say no.

It occurred to Bev, though. "Tell him to get a life," she hissed in Megan's ear. "He's not your type."

"How do you know who's my type?" Megan objected. "Here"—she shoved her stack of books into Bev's unwilling arms—"drop my stuff off when you go past my house, okay? I'll call you later."

But later didn't come for a long, long time. In a way, Megan realized, it never came at all.

# PICKING UP THE PIECES

*Patricia Calvert*

ALADDIN PAPERBACKS

First Aladdin Paperbacks edition January 1999

Copyright © 1993  by Patricia Calvert

Aladdin Paperbacks
An imprint of Simon & Schuster
Children's Publishing Division
1230 Avenue of the Americas
New York, NY 10020

Also available in an Atheneum Books for Young Readers
hardcover edition.
Printed and bound in the United States of America
10 9 8 7 6 5 4 3

The Library of Congress has cataloged
the hardcover edition as follows:
Calvert, Patricia.
Picking up the pieces / Patricia Calvert. — 1st ed.
p.    cm.
Summary: A girl who has suffered a paralyzing spinal cord injury
begins the process of emotional healing.
ISBN 0-684-19558-5 (hc.)
[1. Physically handicapped—Fiction.  2. Self-acceptance—Fiction.]
I. Title.
PZ7.C139Pi   1993    [Fic]—dc20    92-27909
ISBN 0-689-82451-3 (pbk.)

With affection, to
Mary and Lynn Carpenter
and
Larry and Bill Calvert

**1**

Megan watched from the safety of the porch as Mom and Dad finished packing the old, green station wagon. Joey, his pale, spiky hair flying in all directions, created more trouble than he was worth as he darted between and around them, giving advice and trying to help.

Once upon a time, Megan remembered, it *had* been exciting to see what was being taken to the cottage and what was being left behind. Going on vacation every summer had meant a new beginning, a starting over.

Not that Frenchman's Island off the upper Michigan coast was an outpost of civilization, or that a year's worth of provisions had to be taken along when you went there. Truth was, once you got to the lake, it was only another half hour by ferry to the island itself. Just the same, packing to go each year always held the promise of making do and going without, as if they were the Swiss Family Robinson heading off to settle in a wild and dangerous land.

Talk about making do: Once, Megan remembered, the electric popcorn maker got left at home by mistake. "How will we manage?" Mom wailed when she discovered it was missing.

"You mean no popcorn for the whole summer?" Joey cried.

"Aw, c'mon gang, get a grip!" Dad teased, his blue eyes getting crinkly at the corners. Then he showed them how he'd made popcorn when he was a boy visiting his grandparents' farm in Iowa.

First, he melted a golden blob of butter in a cast-iron fry pan, tossed in a handful of yellow kernels, clamped the lid on, then popped the yummiest popcorn ever by shaking the pan vigorously back and forth over the hot wood stove in the kitchen.

Megan sighed and brushed her newly short, sun-colored bangs away from her forehead. Such necessities once made going on vacation seem like a wonderful adventure.

She moved closer to the porch rail and stroked its freshly painted surface. This year, going to Frenchman's Island would be totally different from all those other summers. Among other things, it'd be the first time they'd gone anyplace together since the accident.

This year, it'd be important that certain items not be forgotten or mistakenly left at home. Mom had already made a long list and had checked the items off one by one—antibiotics in case of a bladder infection, catheters, portable toilet, lots of cranberry juice—the kind of stuff that until a few months ago nobody in the family ever needed to worry about.

Yet in spite of everything that had happened, it was still hard to realize they'd never play pioneer on Frenchman's Island again. There'd be no Swiss Family Robinson adventures, no more making do and going without. Packing to go away for the summer would never again be the lighthearted fun it once had been. The accident had changed that for keeps.

**2**

"Dr. Smithson said he thought it might do all of us good to get away for a while," Mom had announced two weeks ago. "So Dad and I talked it over and finally decided the best place we could go would be back to the cottage."

For a moment, Megan couldn't believe what she'd heard.

Go back to the cottage? Just like that, as if nothing had happened, as if things could ever be the same again? How will going back to the island do any of us any good? had been her first thought. Me, in particular? had been the second.

But Joey had jumped up from the supper table and gone whooping around it till finally Dad grabbed him by the belt loops and hollered, "Whoa, tiger! Enough already!"

But hey, who could blame the poor little guy for getting excited? Megan wanted to ask. After all, the last few months had been like a prison sentence for everyone in the family.

During the first few weeks after the accident, life had been narrowed to days and nights at the intensive-care unit in the hospital. Then came consultations with specialists whose names Megan couldn't remember anymore, followed for weeks by endless hours of therapy. No wonder Joey was thrilled by the idea of returning to ordinary life. If Mom and Dad would admit it, they probably were, too.

"Pull that mattress pad back out," Megan heard her father instruct. Mom leaned forward over the tailgate and tugged the mattress, which looked like a humongous foam-rubber egg crate, out of the back of the station wagon.

"I'll stick this in first," Dad announced, hoisting up the collapsible toilet. "Then we'll pack the mattress pad around it."

Megan smiled ruefully. Wow. Times had sure changed; their old pioneer dreams had been replaced by portable potties.

Of course, pioneer dreams weren't the only things that had changed during the past eight months. Before she came home from the rehab unit, for example, the carpet in the living room and hallway had to be torn up to expose the easy-to-wheel-across wood floors underneath. Next, the bathroom on the main floor was remodeled to include a roll-in shower stall with grab bars in place of the elegant Victorian claw-footed bathtub that Mom had always said was worth the price of the old house itself.

But the hardest change of all, Megan remembered, was having to give up her old room upstairs under the eaves. How she'd loved the narrow, twisting, servant's stairway that led up to it, the dormer windows that gave her a private view of the neighbors' gardens and tangled oak woods beyond. She'd treasured the sense that she lived all alone in a garret close to the stars. But the accident changed that too. . . .

Her stuff had to be hauled downstairs into the den, which was smallish and dark and looked out not upon misty Elizabethan woods, but upon the side of the Everleighs' garage, which was the color of carrot soup. Megan didn't ask to have her autographed rock posters or the photo of herself placing first in the eighth-grade three-hundred-yard dash brought down. Such mementos implied a future that didn't belong to her anymore.

When she'd been home awhile, Dad installed ramps at both the front and back porches and painted them blue to match the trim on the house. Everything possible was done to make it easy and convenient to maneuver a wheelchair in and out, up and down.

That became the common denominator of life for the whole family: Will Megan be able to get her wheelchair through? In? Down? Around? Gone forever (*forever* . . . it was such a small word, only seven letters long, a joining of *for* and *ever*, but its true meaning was still too huge for Megan to comprehend) were the days when everything could be taken for granted.

Since the accident, the most ordinary habits required careful planning and time. Tons of time! Going to the bathroom used to be something a person just did; you didn't have to plan for it as if it were a summit conference of foreign nations. Once, it was a function that took moments; now the task could occupy half an hour. If she developed any hint of a bladder infection, it was important to measure her urine to make sure she was excreting enough fluid. And then there were BMs. They'd become a contest between herself and her bowels. Sometimes she didn't win, then had to resort to laxatives and worse yet, enemas. Once, she'd been able to shower and dress in ten minutes flat, now she spent at least forty-five. Her pale hair, not much darker than Joey's, used to hang in a french braid as thick as her wrist between her shoulder blades; last week, Mom cut it all off, super short. Much easier to take care of for the summer, she explained.

"There, that'll ride better," Dad declared as he tucked the mattress pad around the toilet. "I guarantee there'll be no rattling and banging to make us all crazy on the ride up north."

"Yeah, but there's hardly any room left for me and Rollie!" Joey complained loudly. "We used to flake out in back, and there was so much space we could—"

"Don't whine, Joey," Dad warned, and flashed a meaningful glance toward the porch.

Oh, Dad, the little twerp isn't really whining, Megan wished she could explain, and was sorry he'd gotten on Joey's case. Joey was remembering how it had been on other trips to the cottage, when he'd spread a blanket across the whole back end of the station wagon and

7

had played with his Civil War soldiers all the way to Frenchman's Island, his haunches resting agreeably against Rollie's, who snoozed until they'd arrived at their destination.

"That was before, Joey," Mom soothed, taking the sting out of Dad's rebuke. She patted the back of his freckled, birdlike neck. "We all have to remember that things are different now."

Different is hardly the word for it, Megan agreed silently. Life after an SCI—the therapists at the rehab unit glued alphabet labels on everything, including a spinal cord injury—was totally unlike the life that had gone before.

Trouble is, it's just as different for them as it is for me, Megan realized with a familiar guilty pang. The SCI was the reason why Joey and Rollie couldn't hog the whole back end of the station wagon. Why Dad had to build a pair of expensive ramps at the front and back of the house. Why Mom had to give up her beautiful, claw-footed bathtub. Not to mention that it was the reason a garret bedroom under the eaves had to be given back to the stars.

"Hey, you guys, listen up," Megan called softly from her place on the porch. Once again, she stroked the smooth, blueberry-colored porch rail. "It'd really be a lot easier if you three went to the cottage without me. It would, no kidding." Suddenly, the urgent desire to stay home, never to go back to the island with them, burned a hole like a laser beam right through her middle.

"It's not too late to ask Mrs. Adler to come over,"

Megan explained. "She said she would, anytime we needed her, remember?" she reminded the three surprised faces that turned toward her. "Everybody'd have a better time if I stayed right here."

*Be honest*, she wanted to add, *you guys must've already thought about it yourselves.*

"Oh, Meggie!" Mom exclaimed. There was a crisp note of exasperation in her voice. "We've all been together at Frenchman's Island practically since the year one. You were only a baby the first time we went there, and I can't see any reason to change that. Nothing would be the same without you there too."

"But it won't be the same *with* me, either," Megan pointed out.

"It's always been the four of us together at the island," Mom insisted, her voice rising an octave as it always did when she felt uptight, "and that's exactly the way it's going to be this year. Subject closed."

"The five of us," Joey corrected helpfully. "You forgot to count Rollie, Mom."

"Another summer at the cottage won't turn the clock back," Megan warned. But who am I really talking to, she wondered, to Mom and Dad and Joey, or to myself?

She watched as Mom dusted her palms on the fanny of her new stonewashed jeans and approached from the driveway. Her manner indicated there'd be no further discussion about staying home with Mrs. Adler. Funny thing: Mom had never worried much about her appearance, yet had ended up looking younger and prettier than most moms on the block. Her short, gray-blond hair framed her rosy face in feathery curls, and her gray-blue eyes usually had the surprised look of a child. As she trotted up the wheelchair ramp now, however, there was a determined, no-nonsense smile fixed on her lips.

"Give us—and the summer—a chance, Meggie," she urged, and cupped the point of Megan's shoulder in her palm, just as moments before she'd patted Joey's thin little neck. Maybe that's what moms did, Megan decided; no matter how bad things got, they patted people and tried to make them feel better.

"I know what you mean about the clock, sweetie," Mom admitted with a sigh. "You're right; it can't be turned back. Things won't be exactly the same as they were in other years, but nothing ever is, even without, well, accidents. I'm sure if we all try, though, we can make this into another good summer."

**3**

Another good summer . . .

The hope that it might be was so tempting. If only I could have faith again, Megan thought longingly, but grief closed its familiar iron fist around her heart. If only she had the courage to let the summer happen, as summers used to happen. Back then, summers had lives of their own; they simply unfolded and became whatever they were meant to be.

Impossible now, of course. To believe again required the kind of conviction she'd been robbed of eight months ago.

But what had happened eight months ago started out to be only a ten-minute ride home on the buddy seat of Dex Cooper's Yamaha 450. No big deal. It wasn't meant to be a decision that would change her whole life, turn her into a stranger in her own skin, into a person she no longer recognized in the mirror. No; she'd only intended to accept a ride home on a cute guy's motorcycle. So simple. So nearly fatal.

Then, as if that afternoon had been videotaped, Megan pressed Forward and watched the film again, as she had watched it almost every day since the accident.

She'd been studying Dex all fifth hour, never imagining that she'd ever be closer to him than three rows away in Mrs. French's history class. And not really wanting to be, either; after all, as a twelfth-grade transfer student he was a sophisticated Older Man; it was enough merely to watch him, to wonder what kind of a guy he was, to weave romantic dreams around him that didn't have to come true to make her feel warm and fuzzy inside.

Dex had transferred to Hudson High from California the week after school started, and everything about him was West Coasty—his bronze suntan, his streaky yellow hair, his ocean-colored eyes. Every girl at Hudson who had 20/20 vision and a detectable pulse looked at him with awe, so when he wheeled up to the curb that afternoon and suggested in a husky whisper, "Let me give you a lift, babe," it never occurred to Megan to say no.

It occurred to Bev, though. "Tell him to get a life," she hissed in Megan's ear. They'd been walking home together as they'd done almost every afternoon since first grade.

"He's not your type, Meggers," Bev warned. "Liz Baker told me last week that he—"

"How do you know who's my type?" Megan objected, surprising herself even more than Bev. "Good grief, he only wants to give me a ride home, not hold me for ransom. Here"—she shoved her stack of books into Bev's unwilling arms—"drop my stuff off when you go past my house, okay? I'll call you later."

But later didn't come for a long, long time. In a way, Megan realized, it never came at all. When Bev finally showed up at the hospital, there was an accusing, why-didn't-you-listen-to-me? look in her dark eyes. "So anyway, how're you doing?" she'd mumbled, and hadn't wanted to get too close to the bed, as if a spinal cord injury might be contagious. Not that the bed was an ordinary bed; it was a Stryker frame that turned Megan automatically, as if she were on a rotisserie.

"Okay, I guess," Megan remembered whispering, then after a moment, "You still take the same way home we always did, Bev?" Down First Avenue from school, past Mrs. Hammersmith's house on the corner, through the alley behind O'Reilly's, a way that Megan knew she'd never walk again. She'd had to squeeze her eyes shut tight to keep the tears from coming.

Bev only stopped at the hospital one more time. Her second visit was even shorter than the first. She'd hesitated in the doorway before she left, had said, embarrassed, "Well, I suppose it won't be easy to pick up the pieces."

*Pick up the pieces*. As if once I was whole, but now I'm in parts that someone has to put back together, Megan thought, as if I'd turned into Humpty Dumpty. Another thing: It was weird to realize that two people could walk home together every day since forever, trade bubble gum and secrets, yet end up being total strangers to each other because of something called an SCI.

It hurt that Dex Cooper never came at all, even though for a few days he'd been on the same floor at the hospital with a broken leg.

Megan was sure she heard him outside her room one afternoon, asking if visitors were allowed. "Oh, yes," the nurse answered, "and I'll bet she'd be real happy to have company, too." She'd waited and waited, but Dex never came through the door. At Christmastime, someone reported, he went back to live with his dad in California; he had to leave Hudson because of what had happened.

He's the one who's still walking around and I'm the one who'll be in a wheelchair for the rest of my life, but *he* couldn't hack it! Megan thought with fresh disbelief. But on the afternoon when she'd threaded her arms around a waist as narrow as her own, none of that had happened yet. The only thing that mattered was that he was a dish, that tomorrow most of the girls at Hudson would be green-eyed with envy and would want to hear all about it.

"Wanna tool through the park?" Dex had called over his shoulder, the wind peeling the words out of his mouth. She gave his waist an answering squeeze. Less than ten minutes later something went terribly wrong, though now Megan wasn't sure exactly what, not even after playing the video in her mind hundreds of times.

The blacktop ended at the edge of the park, and the road that looped gracefully through the groves of oak and poplar had been laid with fresh pea gravel. Dad explained later that those tiny, smooth, washed stones had probably acted like ball bearings beneath the wheels of the Yamaha. It had been like trying to handle the bike on layers of BB shot, he said.

The Yamaha went into a long, graceful slide. Megan

remembered that she hadn't been scared. Not at first. Then, as if in slow motion, she felt the machine rise under her like a willful beast and claw its way into the air. It turned sideways against the bronze October sun . . . the scarlet and gold trees in the park flew upside down . . . then she landed hard on the fresh-mown grass at the edge of the road.

At first, it seemed merely that the breath had been knocked out of her. She took several deep, thirsty gulps of air. Slowly, Megan realized that she felt rather odd. It was as if there were a line drawn just below her belly button, beyond which the rest of her body felt, well, elsewhere. It was like the feeling she got in her lips after she'd had a shot of Novocaine at the dentist's, a queer there-but-not-there feeling.

She'd raised her head off the grass and peered down at her body. I'm okay, thank God, she assured herself, relieved. Her feet and legs were still there, the toes of her Nikes pointing like a pair of white arrows toward the sky. Then, lifting her head again and staring at her feet, she realized, *But I can't feel them*. Can't feel them! There was no sensation either in her ankles . . . or knees . . . or hips. Numb; everything was numb. But the feeling would come back as soon as she got her breath, right? Yes, yes, yes. Except that it never did.

Now, Megan felt Mom lean close and heard her whisper, "Remember how piney-winey the air smells on the island, Meggie?" She felt her mother's strong fingers knead her shoulder, pulling her away from the video that she'd been rerunning in her head.

"Did Dad tell you he arranged for Mr. Hassler to

build a wheelchair ramp that goes all the way down to the beach? You can go down to the water anytime you want. When you were little you played down there by the hour, remember, Megan?''

*Remember, remember!* Mom seemed to plead. Megan shrugged her shoulder from beneath her mother's fingers.

"Of course I remember," she announced flatly. "I haven't lost my memory, Mom, only my legs." It wasn't the first time they'd had one of these conversations. Why couldn't Mom quit trying to make things better when there was no way they ever could be?

Actually, it'd be best if I couldn't remember, Megan wished she could explain. That way, she'd never be able to compare then to now. Besides, what did it matter what the air smelled like on Frenchman's Island? Islands were meant for people who could swim and fish and water-ski; islands weren't meant for people who couldn't do any of those things anymore.

"Joey," Mom called, giving Megan's shoulder a final hopeful squeeze, "get Rollie's leash, will you? And find Rollie while you're at it. We ought to get going as soon as we can." She vanished inside the house, where Megan could hear her going from room to room, checking to see that all the windows were closed, that nothing on her list had been overlooked.

Megan wheeled herself down the ramp, which was painted the color of blueberries just like the new porch rail, then rolled around the corner of the house into the backyard. The new sidewalk and the new patio were

16

supersmooth too. The old ones had been made out of blue and gray flagstone, beautiful to look at but too bumpy to wheel a chair easily across.

"None of them want to admit it," Megan confided to the empty backyard, "but it's true. They *would* have a better time without me. If I stayed here, the three of them could do all the stuff the four of us used to do together. After a while, they'd be having such a good time that they wouldn't even miss me."

To be honest, she wasn't thinking only of them. "It'd be easier for me, too," she admitted to the grass, the lilac bush, the willow tree. With the three of them gone and no one around to nag her, she'd stay in her room all day. She'd read books and listen to her favorite tapes and write in the journal that Gram had given her at Christmas. Mrs. Adler could come over several times a day, just to look in and make sure everything was okay. Yes, it would be easier, hassle free, no pretending.

That's why home study was so great, Megan realized. It meant she'd never have to go back to Hudson again. Would never have to worry about not getting into the john on time and maybe having an accident in the hall. Gross! It was appalling to imagine how she'd feel if something like that happened in front of everybody.

Merely thinking about it made Megan's cheeks flame. No, no; better never to take a chance. Better to do homework via the TV hookup, to let Mom carry the finished lessons back and forth to school, than to be a spectacle, to have her friends stare at her with embarrassment and pity. Home study was perfect because it meant she'd never have to pretend to be someone she'd never be again.

Megan braced her palms on the padded armrests of her chair and hoisted her buttocks off the seat. It was something she had to do three or four times every hour, the therapists said, to take the pressure off her ischial bones. Ischial bones; until the accident, she never knew she had any; now she had to worry about developing pressure sores on her rear end.

As she lowered herself onto the seat again, Megan spied Rollie arriving home through a hole in the back fence. His front paws were dirty up to his elbows, a sure sign he'd been digging in somebody's garden again.

"*Ba-a-ad* Rollie!" she scolded softly. "One of these days the neighbors will haul you off to the dog pound and forget to tell us where they took you." Rollie threw himself on the grass near the wheel of her chair and hid his freckled spaniel face against his telltale paws.

"Quit with the dramatics," Megan advised. "You're not trying out for a part in a Disney movie, chum. Anyway, I was only kidding." Rollie peeked up and wiggled his nub of a tail, happy to be forgiven. Megan watched him tear around to the front of the house and relished the feel of early-morning sunshine on the back of her neck. She turned her chair so that the sunlight slanted in golden bars across her knees, but she felt no sensation of warmth caress them.

She leaned forward to massage the calf of each leg through her jeans. The flesh she touched seemed to belong to someone she didn't know. Her legs felt as unreal as the plastic legs of a Barbie doll.

18

"Megan?" Mom called from the front porch. Megan blinked back her tears but didn't answer. The terrible strangeness of her body still shocked her. A moment later, she heard Mom lock the front door. "Go find Megan, Joey," Mom asked with a sigh, "and tell her we're ready to leave. If we get going now we'll be at Frenchman's Island by lunchtime." It was only seven-thirty, but Megan heard a note of weariness in her mother's voice.

Joey's running footsteps echoed around the corner of the house. "C'mon, Megan," he cried, "it's time to go!" His nine-year-old voice was filled with blue and gold summer dreams. He grabbed the arm of her chair and jiggled it emphatically.

"Guess what?" he demanded, and leaned close, his sweet-sour breath warming her cheek. "Dad says he'll try to lease the cottage for the whole summer. We might be able to stay till school starts, just like we did before—" He stopped, and his expression turned from glee to one of fear and shame. Megan knew he was remembering the scolding he'd gotten from Dad only moments ago.

"Hey, Megan, I didn't mean—"

"No problem, Joey," she assured him quickly. She patted his hand; they'd had waffles with syrup for breakfast, and his fingers were still sticky. "It's okay; I know what you meant."

She did, too. Other years, she'd dreamed all winter long about going to the island as soon as school got out. Dad always tried to lease the same cottage on the south side of the island, and on the ride up there each year, she'd made a mental list of all the places she'd visit as soon as they arrived: that secret place deep in the woods where there was a clear spring; the worn raft in the middle of the lake; best of all, the Hideout.

This year, she wouldn't make a list.

A peculiar heaviness settled over Megan. Going back to such favorite places could only be done by the girl-who-used-to-be, not the girl-who-was. It was her spinal cord (Megan often imagined that it had been silver and thin as a spider's web, yet strong enough to suspend a thousand dreams) that had linked her to that old life, those old places. When that thin, silver cord had been snapped, she'd been cut loose from herself. From Mom and Dad and Joey. From Hudson High. From Bev. From life.

"Not fair, not fair!" Megan cried softly. Just because on a bronze October afternoon she'd hopped onto the buddy seat of a cute guy's motorcycle and an accident had happened that nobody could make unhappen—*not fair, not fair!*

She'd only agreed to accept a ride home. She'd never suspected it'd mean she'd never play basketball again. Swim again. Slow dance again with a boy she liked. It wasn't supposed to mean she'd spend the rest of her life being someone she'd never intended to be.

**4**

Megan wheeled herself through the doorway of the cottage and braked her chair in the middle of the living room.

She closed her eyes and took a deep sniff of the room's tantalizing, musty smell. It was as if the mingled odors of mouse droppings and darkness had been hoarded through the dim months of winter, so that when the first visitor opened the door the cottage could sigh, "Now let summer begin!"

Megan blinked and sniffed again. She felt a rush of gladness that she hadn't stayed home with Mrs. Adler after all.

Mom dashed about, sweeping the flowered curtains aside so that bright noontime sunshine splashed everywhere, throwing windows open to the piney-winey air. Joey didn't bother to come indoors; he'd jumped out of the car the moment they arrived and had raced down to the water's edge. Rollie didn't stop there but flung him-

21

self into the lake, where now he was paddling around in giddy circles, barking deliriously. Last summer (that ancient lifetime ago), Megan had been right down there with them.

"We'll put you on the porch this year, Meggie," Mom called over her shoulder. The announcement was another reminder that although the cottage smelled as it used to, that although Joey and Rollie were doing what they always did, certain things could not be the same at all.

"It's close to everything," Mom explained, as if an explanation were needed. "To the kitchen, you know, and the shower and stuff. And with luck the septic system won't plug up this year, which will mean we three won't have to run up the hill to the outhouse, and you won't have to use that portable potty even once."

Mom marched briskly past onto the porch, her tennies chirping on the painted floor, and flung open the windows that overlooked the beach. "Did I tell you that I remembered to bring the binoculars?" she asked brightly. Too brightly, Megan realized. "So that even when you can't be on the beach you can keep track of what's going on down there."

"Great," Megan answered vaguely, not convinced that binoculars would help or hurt. When Mom whisked by on her return to the kitchen, Megan rolled slowly onto the porch herself.

It wasn't a large room, but with three walls filled with windows, it seemed airier and more spacious than she remembered. She could see the mainland across the lake, a ribbon of several shades of green threaded between the blue of the sky and the darker blue of the water. To the east was the cottage that the Chambliss family rented every summer; to the west was a faint green blot far out in the lake that was the Hideout.

All of the white wicker furniture had been moved out of the porch, and in the center of the room stood a metal hospital bed. Other summers, she'd slept in the small back bedroom with Joey, always on the top bunk because sometimes he walked in his sleep.

No more top bunks for her, of course. Next to the hospital bed stood a wheeled cart to hold medicines and fruit juices and her alarm clock. The braided rug that once brightened the painted floor of the porch had been rolled up and was propped upright, like a log, in the corner behind the door.

"Where'd you get the bed?" Megan wondered aloud.

"Mr. Hassler brought it from the mainland when he came over last month to build the new ramp down to the beach," Mom hollered from the kitchen. "We're renting it by the week from a medical supply company over there."

Makes sense, Megan agreed wordlessly. After all, why get one for the whole season when nobody knew yet how it would work out, this business of trying to create another summer that was as good as all the others?

"Does it look okay, Meggie?" Mom called anxiously.

"A hospital bed is a hospital bed, Mom," Megan answered dryly. As such, it hardly needed to make a fashion statement; it merely had to be functional, to be of the right height to make wheelchair transfers easy.

Through the open porch windows, Megan saw Joey running toward the cottage with Rollie, wet and soggy, in hot pursuit. "C'mon, Megan!" he cried when he saw her peering out. "The new ramp's great—you're gonna be able to come right down to the lake any time you want, just like always!"

Not quite like always, Megan disagreed silently. "I'll come down tomorrow, Joey," she called back. "Right now I'm sorta pooped from the trip."

It wasn't quite the truth. Actually, the journey had been much less tiring than she'd been afraid it would be. The problem was that she just didn't want to get out there and try the new ramp, not yet. Tomorrow would be soon enough. She might have a whole summer of tomorrows to spend. But Joey was too happy to be disappointed by her cop-out; he was already on his way back to the lake, his winter-white legs flashing like silver blades in the June sun. This time when Rollie hurled himself into the water, Joey belly flopped in behind him.

"Okay if we have grilled cheese sandwiches for lunch?" Mom wanted to know. "And tomato soup too?"

"Sure, Mom," Megan answered. Cheese sandwiches and tomato soup were what they always ate for lunch on the first day at the cottage; Mom was asking just to have something ordinary to talk about, Megan knew. Later, in the middle of the afternoon, she'd make s'mores for a snack because supper wouldn't be served until everything had been cleaned and put away, when the sun had gone down and the lake was the color of melted amethysts.

Joey had to be coaxed out of the water when lunch was ready, his nose and the points of his shoulders already rosy with sunburn. When they were halfway through their tomato soup, however, Dad had an announcement that caused Joey to turn pale.

"Hate to be the one to have to drop this news on you, champ," he said, "but the Chamblisses won't be coming up this summer."

"How come?" Joey yelped, and dropped his cheese sandwich onto his plate as if it didn't taste good anymore. "It won't be any fun without Danny Chambliss! I won't have anybody to play with—not nobody!" He was as mournful as if he'd been told Danny was never coming back, ever.

Dad shrugged sympathetically. "Sorry about that, Joey. But the Pritchards over on the other side of the island will be here next week. They've got twins about your age, remember?" He winked, as if he believed the news would cheer Joey up. "Hey, maybe that means you'll have twice the fun," he joked.

Joey was not amused. "One of the Pritchards is a girl and the other one's a dork," he grumbled.

"So what happened to the Chamblisses this year?" Mom wanted to know, and poured a second round of milk for everyone. "Joey's not the only one who's disappointed," she admitted. "I'll miss Sallie; she always came on vacation with loads of recipes to swap. It was

25

fun trying them out with her right next door in case I goofed up.''

"I met Ernie Chambliss at the bank a day or so before we left," Dad explained. "He told me he's on sabbatical from the university and is taking the whole family to Europe while he researches a new book. He said he'd heard the place next door had been leased for the summer, though, so it's not as if we'll be totally neighborless.''

Joey retrieved his sandwich. "Maybe they'll have kids," he speculated, "ones who aren't girls or dorks.''

Dad shook his head. "Better not get your hopes up, champ," he advised. "Mr. Hassler told me on the phone that an older couple have taken the place. Said the fellow was a mellow old soul but that his wife was a real barn burner.''

"A what?" Mom choked. "What, may I ask, is a barn burner?''

Dad grinned slyly. "I think Mr. Hassler meant to imply she's a character. He told me she wore enough fake gold jewelry to sink her to the bottom of the lake if she ever fell in. According to him, her hair is dyed the color of iodine, so she must be quite a sight.''

"Ummm," Mom murmured, and set out dishes for lemon sherbet. "As soon as we get completely settled, I'll invite them over.''

Megan listened absentmindedly. It didn't break her heart to hear that the Chambliss family had made other plans for the summer. Knowing that lovely Lisa would be far away in Europe was a big relief.

Ah, Lisa! She of the long, brown legs, whose favorite pastime was the polishing, grooming, and beautifying of L. Chambliss. No way was she my favorite person before the accident, so for sure I wouldn't be crazy about her now, Megan reflected. In summers past, Lisa turned herself all day like a pig on a spit—looking spectacularly unpiglike, of course—and when she did rouse herself enough to water-ski behind her dad's boat, she looked like someone in an ad for suntan lotion. Having two old gaffers next door, even if one of them was weird, would be perfect.

When lunch was over, Megan wheeled herself to the sink. Lucky that the cottage was old and that the cabinets were lower than in modern homes, Megan thought as she washed the dishes Mom had stacked up. She used to hate doing kitchen stuff; now she didn't mind because it was one thing she still could do. Next, Mom spent all afternoon cleaning cupboards. Then she fussed until she fit all the white wicker porch furniture into the living room so skillfully that the room didn't even look crowded. At last, it was time to start supper.

"Want to dredge the chicken in flour for me?" Mom invited. I used to hate cooking, too, Megan mused; that wasn't boring anymore, either. She wheeled herself to the fridge, took out a package of chicken, and washed the pieces in cold water. She patted them dry on paper towels, then rolled each piece in seasoned flour that Mom had mixed up.

"I'll have to take Dad down to the ferry in the morning so he can catch the train back to the city," Mom said, and sighed, brushing a wisp of hair away from her damp cheek. She made the announcement as if it were weighted with special significance.

Megan stiffened in her chair. "So?" she asked. "That's how Dad usually gets to the ferry, Mom. You take him down there."

"Well . . ." Mom hesitated before going on. "It means that you and Joey will be here alone till I get back."

"Don't start up with that, Mom," Megan warned. "You've left us alone here dozens of times. Anyway, it's only fifteen minutes down to the ferry and fifteen minutes back. What's the big deal?" Megan struggled to keep her voice level.

"That's true, Meggie, but I've never left you alone since—"

Since the accident, Megan knew Mom intended to say. She floured the last piece of chicken. Beginning eight months ago, everything had to be dated SA, Since the Accident.

"There has to be a first time for everything," Megan pointed out. She laid the pieces of chicken in the electric fry pan, where they sizzled noisily, matching the sizzle she felt inside.

"But I'm not sure if I should . . ." Mom tried to finish, but again her voice trailed off uncertainly.

"Well, *I* am, Mom," Megan insisted, aware of the sharp note in her own voice. "You and Dad are the ones who are always talking about real life. That's what you said going back to Hudson was—facing real life, you said. Taking Dad to the ferry is real life, too, so just do it, okay?'' As the chicken began to brown, she turned each piece in the pan and studiously kept her glance from meeting her mother's.

"Okay, Meggie," Mom agreed at last, without conviction. "I suppose it'll be all right."

I ought to apologize to her for being so cranky, Megan realized. She knew she'd spoken too sharply. Again. Been too defensive. Again. Just the same, something deep down inside her wouldn't let her take the words back. Not now, not yet.

The thing was, the whole family talked about real life, yet no one agreed on exactly what it was. To Mom and Dad it was going back to Hudson, yet staying at the cottage alone for a measly half hour while Dad was driven down to the ferry was considered too reckless to be considered. Megan drained the last two pieces of crisp, golden-brown chicken on paper towels.

But I'll apologize later, she vowed. If I can.

That night, alone on the front porch, Megan decided it might be sort of neat to sleep there by herself while everyone else was tucked away at the back of the cottage.

A feeling crept over her that was very much like the one she'd had when she'd lived in her garret room close to the stars, a feeling of belonging to herself. Alone like this at night, sometimes the California-cool face of Dex Cooper floated in front of her in the darkness and she asked: Why, Dex? Why didn't you come to see me? Why didn't you call? Send flowers, a card? Something?

Megan laid her palm across her heart to ease its ache

and tried to concentrate instead on familiar night sounds. Outside, the leaves of the poplar trees pressed softly against the windows, yet she could still see the faint pulse of stars in the dark summer sky beyond. Mom had left one of the windows open, and through it Megan heard water lightly kiss the sandy beach. Birds murmured sleepily in the pine trees behind the cottage. She propped herself on her elbows so she could get a goodnight peek at the lake.

A few feet away, a door closed softly at the Chambliss cottage. A moment later, Megan heard the sound of footsteps on the dock next door.

She fumbled for the switch that raised the head of her bed. The motor under it purred obediently, lifting her upright. Good; now maybe she'd get a glimpse of that old woman whose hair was reported to be the color of iodine. In the pale amber glow of the Chambliss dock light, however, Megan saw no elderly lady burdened with enough gold bangles to sink her to the bottom of the lake.

The person who walked slowly to the end of the pier was young and had a pair of legs as long and straight as Lisa Chambliss's.

"Just my luck," Megan groaned under her breath. "There goes the summer, I guess." The stranger next door faded into the evening gloom at the end of the dock and stood there in the mild, silver light of the stars. Megan squinted hard and wished she could see better.

But why do I want to torture myself? she wondered. Looking at tall, straight-legged people who could walk was like picking at a scab: You knew you shouldn't do it, but you did it anyway, till finally you began to bleed.

Nevertheless, she rummaged in the dark for the binoculars Mom had laid on the medicine cart. She held them up to her eyes and fumbled with the focusing device.

It wasn't a girl who stood at the end of the Chambliss dock. It was a boy. Megan tried not to breathe and studied him carefully. His hair was barely long enough to be caught at the nape of his neck and fastened in a ponytail that was about the length of a crooked finger. He stood with his hands rammed into the pockets of his white nylon Windbreaker and rocked lightly back and forth on his heels. As she watched, he took something out of his right pocket.

Whatever it was, he inspected it for a moment, then pitched it into the lake, where it made a musical *plink-plink*. He turned, shoulders slouched, and returned to the darkened cottage. He let himself in the side door and switched on the light above the kitchen sink. Feeling like a spy in a movie, Megan watched as he filled a glass with water and took a long, thoughtful drink. He reached for the light switch and flicked it off, vanishing as surely as if she'd only imagined him.

Megan set the binoculars on the medicine cart and lowered the head of her bed until she was stretched out flat again. Had Mr. Hassler been mistaken about who'd rented the cottage next door? And what had the stranger just pitched into the water?

Megan stared into the darkness. Maybe he had a girl-friend who'd just dumped him; maybe it was the class ring she'd returned to him that he'd pitched into the lake a moment ago. Bev had dumped Randy Berryman last year; he said she'd broken his heart and he'd never get over it. Maybe the guy next door was heartbroken, too. When he threw his ring away he'd whispered: "I'll love you forever, Monica," and now it was winking and glittering in the oozy silt, attracting the admiration of turtles and fishes.

Megan smiled in the dark. Your imagination's in over-drive, lady, she told herself ruefully. Just the same, there was something about the stranger next door that troubled her. Standing alone at the end of the Chambliss dock he'd reminded her of someone—but who? Then she knew.

*Me,* Megan realized.

"Yeah, me," she breathed softly into the darkness. "He looked like he's a person who's searching for something. Something he lost, maybe, like I lost the me in me." Had he come to Frenchman's Island this summer thinking he might find it?

For the first time since the accident, Megan felt a tingle of curiosity. For eight months, she hadn't thought about anything except *my* legs, *my* bladder, *my* pressure sores, *my* spine (that beautiful, broken spider web), but now—

Megan brought herself up short.

Now what? A chill settled over her that had nothing to do with the cool night air wafting through the open porch window. Nothing about the summer had really changed, she reminded herself. Tomorrow she would still be in a wheelchair and he, whoever he was, would still have two long, straight legs that could carry him anywhere he wanted to go. Megan's curiosity, which a moment before had been as bright as a spark from a campfire, flickered, then died.

**5**

Megan didn't hear the station wagon leave the driveway the next morning. When she opened her eyes, the cottage seemed so unnaturally silent that for a split second she was seized with panic. She raised herself on her elbows, her heart hammering in her chest, then saw with relief that Joey, still in his pj's, was already down on the beach, throwing a Frisbee for Rollie.

She eased herself back onto her egg-crate mattress, her panic receding like a wave leaving the shore. Wide-eyed, she blinked at the ceiling. *I'm all alone,* she realized slowly. All alone . . .

It made her feel—Megan searched for the right phrase—well, like a person again, she decided, rather than a patient. Who would ever think that being a patient twenty-four hours a day would be such hard work? But it was, especially when the worst thing that'd ever kept you down before was a bad cold.

Once upon a time, she'd imagined that *patient* meant

someone who was almost dying or was old and in a nursing home, like Grandpa Murphy had been after he had his final surgery. But she was neither one, not dying and not old. On the other hand, those other two words— *disabled* and *handicapped*—weren't words that told the truth about her, either. The big question still was: What *was* the truth about her now?

Megan closed her eyes and savored her solitude, knowing that Mom would be back soon and these precious moments of independence would vanish. For an instant, she felt almost happy, so when Joey's scream came through the open window it was as painful and shocking as if a knife had been plunged into her chest.

"Mega-a-an," he shrieked, "come quick! Something terrible just happened to Rollie!"

Once you'd had an SCI, though, there was no way you could ever do anything quickly again. Just the same, Megan grabbed her transfer board off the medicine cart and positioned it at a slant against the seat of her chair. She scooted herself toward the edge of the bed and leaned across the chair with a hand braced on each padded armrest. She dragged her buttocks across the smooth sheet onto the board, then let herself slide down its incline into the chair. She leaned forward, placed each foot on its footrest, fastened a strap across each instep, then rolled toward the kitchen door.

"What's the matter, Joey?" she called, peering through the screen. She half expected to look out and see something ghastly, but instead she saw only that Rollie was standing glumly in the shallow water, the blue Frisbee floating idly nearby. Joey crouched at Rollie's side, his face wet with tears.

"He's hurt bad, Megan," Joey wailed. "And he's ble-eeding!" Only then did Megan notice that the water around Rollie's front feet was slowly turning the color of tomato juice.

She reached across the kitchen counter and plucked a dish towel off the drying rack next to the sink, then wheeled herself outside onto the landing. She stopped short and stared, dismayed, at the new ramp leading down to the lake's edge. She'd made excuses all day yesterday not to go outside to inspect it, but here it was, as forbiddingly long as the runway for a Concord jet.

Look, chum, you're the one who lectured Mom yesterday about real life, Megan reminded herself. Okay, this is it, Real Life with capital letters. The ramps at home weren't so daunting, being rather short, while this one had to be at least fifty or sixty feet long. She felt her armpits dampen with anxiety.

"Hurry up, Megan!" Joey begged. "Hurry!"

Megan gritted her teeth and started to roll slowly toward him. She kept the brake on her chair set just tightly enough to keep herself from descending too fast. She had to admit one thing: Mr. Hassler had done a super job on the ramp, because the trip down to the water's edge was as smooth as the one across the new concrete patio at home.

"Help Rollie get out of the water," Megan ordered when she got almost to the end of the ramp, "so we can take a better look at his paws." We? Not quite; Joey would have to be the one who did all the checking.

"C'mon, Rollie," Joey coaxed. Rollie hung his head and refused to budge.

"C'mon, ol' buddy," Joey pleaded, sniffling harder as the water around Rollie's feet turned redder. Finally, Rollie limped up the beach, his nose almost touching the sand, as mortified as if he'd been caught doing something naughty again. He left bright pink footprints with each step he took.

"Lift up one of his paws, Joey," Megan suggested, pointing at Rollie's front feet. "Can you see anything?"

Joey knelt on the sand beside Rollie and picked up his left front foot. "Oh, jeez, Megan, he's wounded real bad!" he howled, and began to cry even louder. "There's this great big gash right in the middle of—"

"Stay cool, Joey," Megan urged, and ripped the dish towel lengthwise, then into fourths. She held one of the wide white strips out to her brother. "Take this, Joey. Wrap it around Rollie's foot. When you're done, do his other paw, too. Make the bandages snug but not too tight. At least that'll keep his feet from bleeding too much until we can—"

She hadn't finished her instructions when she heard the soft hiss of tires in the sand in front of the cottage. Mom leaped out of the station wagon and came down the ramp at a dead run, hair flying, face white.

"Oh, my God, Meggie, are you all right?"

"It's not me, Mom," Megan soothed. "It's only Rollie."

"*Only* Rollie?" Joey moaned, his voice blurry with tears. "He's practically dying, and all you can say is *only* Rollie?"

"He cut his feet somehow," Megan tried to explain. She wished she'd been able to jump out of her chair to inspect Rollie firsthand, but only the old Megan, the one who hadn't gotten on Dex Cooper's motorcycle, could've done that.

Mom unwrapped Joey's lumpy bandage and peered at Rollie's paw herself. Rollie, beginning to enjoy the attention, brightened and sniffed at his foot with interest. "Oh, dear," Mom said with a sigh, "the cut seems to be quite nasty. I think it's more than I know how to take care of myself. I wonder what we should—"

"There's that retired veterinarian on the far side of the island," Megan reminded her. "We took Rollie over there a couple of years ago, remember, after he chased the porcupine and got all those quills in his nose."

Mom nodded. "Oh, yes, you're right. I suppose that's the best thing to do—" But instead of hurrying off, she continued to hold Rollie's paw. "We might be gone quite a while, though, so maybe you ought to get ready to come with us, Meggie."

"Hey, Mom," Megan began, a familiar tight ache settling in her jaw, "it's no big hairy deal, no pun intended. I'll be okay right here. You can call me from the vet's if you think it's going to take more than an hour to get him fixed up." She stared at her mother's hand, which now looked as if it were covered thickly with catsup. "But you guys better get going before the poor pooch bleeds to death."

The mention of blood and death raised a fresh howl from Joey. Together, he and Mom partly coaxed and partly carried Rollie up the beach to the waiting station

38

wagon. It took both of them, pushing and hoisting, to load him into the back, then they were off to Dr. Myles's on the opposite side of the island.

When they finally disappeared around the bend in the road, Megan sank back in her chair. Talk about real life! This was a little more real than anything she had in mind. She glanced furtively toward the Chambliss cottage. Thank heavens Joey's caterwauling hadn't roused the new neighbors.

Megan turned to face the lake. She was alone again. Really alone this time.

She let her chair roll slowly to the very end of Mr. Hassler's smooth new ramp. All by herself, she felt brave enough to do something she wouldn't have done with anyone looking on. A mixture of dread and anticipation made her chest feel tight, forcing her to hesitate a moment. The rising wind teased the lake into whitecaps, and the waves inching up the beach were as foamy as soapsuds.

Screwing up her courage, Megan locked the brake on her chair. She loosened the Velcro strap across the instep of her right foot, then let her foot drop onto the sand. A wave bubbled across the beach, brushed her toes, receded, then swept back and covered her foot.

She should have known: Although the water was cold and her toes ought to have recoiled from the chill, she felt no sensation at all. Not of wetness or cold or grittiness of sand. Nothing. The water might as well have been washing over someone else's foot. Barbie's, maybe.

Hadn't the counselors at the rehab unit warned her

what moments such as this would bring? Oh, yes. Grief. Pain. She would mourn, they told her, for what could never be felt again.

*Poor toes!* Megan cried silently. *Poor foot! Poor Meggie!* She felt compelled to seize her foot, kiss it back to life, rub warmth and sensation back into it. Instead, she bent and lifted it off the sand (it was limp, white, cold, like a dead fish), and placed it back on its footrest. As she did so, a shadow fell across the sand. Megan froze, unable to glance upward.

Please, no visitors, she begged wordlessly. Whoever you are, just go on about your own business, okay? Leave me alone; I don't want company, and most especially I don't want sympathy. If she kept her head bent, maybe whoever was standing there would just turn around and—

"Hi."

The voice above was ordinary, neither high nor low, neither friendly nor unfriendly. Most definitely, though, it was a boy's voice.

"Hi," Megan, still crouched over her knees, whispered against her shinbone.

"You're practically the first human being I've seen since we got here two weeks ago," the voice confided. "I figured I might end up doing a Robinson Crusoe shtick all summer long."

Don't expect now that you've found me that I'll be your Friday, Megan was tempted to warn. She kept her head down, then heard a swish of bare feet in the sand.

"Was that your dog I saw out here a little while ago?" the voice inquired.

"Yeah," Megan mumbled. If she continued to speak only in monosyllables, maybe he'd get the idea he wasn't welcome and would bug off.

"He must've cut his foot, right?"

"Right."

"I think I know how it happened. I saw him run over there"—the shadow of an arm pointed like an arrow across the sand—"where some dummy had left a broken Pepsi bottle. I think your mutt must've stepped on it. Guess I should've picked it up the first time I noticed it."

"Oh." Joey definitely would not be thrilled to hear Rollie referred to as a mutt. Megan didn't try to fill the silence that followed. The wind continued to sigh in the treetops, and the waves scrubbed the beach with their foamy suds. The silence deepened. Surely this guy would get the message and would decide to—

"So anyway, my name's Harris St. John," the voice above offered hopefully.

Harris St. John? It sounded like the name of a successful stockbroker, an old guy who carried an eelskin briefcase and got chauffeured to work in a long, black car with smoked windows.

"What's yours?"

Megan didn't answer right away. "Megan," she finally admitted in a tiny voice.

"Megan Megan?" The voice had a smile in it. "You probably have a last name, right?"

"Murphy." He was prying more out of her than she'd intended to part with.

"Megan Murphy. Ummm. The M and M girl—but I

bet you're not the kind who melts in anybody's hand, right?''

Smart alecks who make feeble jokes I can do without, Megan thought resentfully. The shadow moved across the sand until it was pointed at her like a needle on a compass. Megan adjusted her glance enough to see a pair of bare, brown feet attached to two skinny legs. Unwilling to look any further upward, she inspected Harris St. John's kneecaps. They were knobby, and on the right one there was a small, white, half-moon scar.

"You gonna be here all summer?" Harris inquired.

"I don't think so," Megan lied.

The bare feet shuffled in the sand. "Well, maybe until you leave we can, you know, do stuff together," Harris suggested.

Do stuff together? Was he blind or what? Megan straightened herself abruptly. This guy was as big a dork as Joey thought Billy Pritchard was.

"I hardly think so," she replied coolly. "See, there's not a lot I can do anymore." She hadn't noticed last night that he wore glasses. Not sexy, tinted, aviator-style glasses like dudes wore, but small, round, apothecary's glasses such as John Lennon had worn. The eyes behind the thick lenses were mild and blue.

"Anymore?" Harris's glance flickered across the armrests of her chair. "But I bet you play checkers," he said brightly, in that same too-bright voice that Mom often used, the let's-be-nice-to-Megan tone of voice.

"Well, I—" The truth was it used to be one of her favorite things to do at the cottage in the summer. A year ago she'd gotten so good that she'd beaten Dad nearly every time they'd played.

"Yeah, we could do that," Harris pressed, seeing her hesitation. He smiled, showing two large, front teeth that made him look like a bespectacled rabbit.

Megan struggled to get her chair turned around for the trip up the ramp. The incline wasn't steep, but she had to stroke her handrims hard to get going. Harris wisely didn't offer to help but walked politely alongside after she got rolling.

"Like, you know, maybe we could play tomorrow," he persisted. "How about if I come over in the afternoon?"

By the time she got to the top of the landing, Megan was too out of breath to object. She fumbled with the latch on the kitchen door, struggled to hold it open while she manuevered herself inside, then let the door snap shut behind her. As soon as she was on the other side of the screen she felt better, knowing that Harris St. John couldn't study her too closely.

"What d'you say?" he asked from his side of the screen.

This guy's like the snapping turtle that caught Joey by the big toe a couple of summers ago, Megan decided. Once he gets hold of you, he just won't let go. "Well, maybe," she agreed, and hoped that he'd notice her lack of enthusiasm. With any luck, by tomorrow he'd forget his turtle ways and stay next door where he belonged.

"Great!" Harris declared. "See ya later, M and M," he called. He hopped nimbly off the landing, then loped off toward the Chambliss cottage, whistling happily to himself.

Alone in the kitchen, Megan patted the arms of her chair. The emptiness of the cottage that only half an hour earlier had seemed so delicious now seemed lonesome. She looked at the clock above the stove. Mom and Joey had been gone almost forty-five minutes already. She wondered how Rollie was, if the vet had to take stitches in his paws. She hoisted herself off her ischial bones, then eased back into her chair.

Maybe she'd wait in her bedroom for Mom and Joey to come back. Megan wheeled slowly onto the porch. Next door, the Chambliss cottage seemed deserted; Harris had vanished, and the drapes were drawn securely across all the windows. She couldn't decide if she was sorry she'd more or less agreed to play a game of checkers tomorrow. Harris St. John had been so insistent that it had been easier to say maybe rather than no.

Megan rested her palms on her unfeeling knees. Back home in Hudson, there'd been no use pretending things would ever be the same after the accident. Back there, everyone knew she'd never be Megan the Magnificent again, the blond bombshell who had spurred the girl's basketball team to its first-ever victory over the River Falls Rockettes.

But here on Frenchman's Island it was quite different, Megan reflected. The only me that Harris St. John will ever know is the one he met on the beach today, the me who's in a wheelchair. She hugged herself lightly. Deep inside, something stirred, stretched, and sighed as if it had been sleeping too long in the dark.

Could I start over here? Megan asked herself.

Would this be a good place to pick up the pieces, like Bev said I'd have to do? Is this the place to try, this summer on Frenchman's Island with a person named Harris St. John, who wears funny glasses and has rabbity front teeth and who doesn't know anything about the me who used to be?

# 6

"So anyway, how's that pooch of yours doing today?" Megan overheard Harris ask Joey.

She shoved herself quickly away from the screen door and prayed that he hadn't caught a glimpse of her peeking out. To be caught looking for him after he'd decided not to show his face for two days would make it seem as if she cared whether he showed up or not. A couple of days ago, picking up the pieces had seemed worth thinking about; now that she'd had time to reconsider, however, Megan recognized the idea for exactly what it had been—a foolish summer fantasy.

In fact, when Harris hadn't come over yesterday, either, Megan felt almost relieved and understood what probably had happened: He'd gotten back to the Chambliss cottage after their encounter on the beach, and he too began to have second thoughts about starting anything up. Someone in a wheelchair? "Hey, who needs it? Too much of a hassle," he might've said to himself. "Forget it; wait till a better idea comes along!"

So if he doesn't care, why should I? Megan had concluded. I never wanted to play checkers with him anyhow. I only said maybe to get him off my case.

Outside, she heard Joey reply, "Rollie's okay. The vet put in a few stitches, the kind that come out by themselves. Gave us some goop in a tube, too," he went on eagerly, "and we hafta smear it on Rollie's paws at night before he goes to bed." There was a brief pause, and Megan knew all too well the shrewd look in her brother's eyes as he sized Harris up.

"You must be the guy my sister said wants to play checkers with her," he observed with customary bluntness. "She told us you were gonna come over a couple of days ago."

Great. Swell. Joey made it sound as if she'd moped around the whole time waiting for Harris to show his face. It wasn't my idea in the first place, she wanted to yell at both of them, and anyway I only said maybe! Just because it was an accident (and for sure she didn't need another one of those) that Harris was on the island this summer, and that he was the only other person around who was her age, didn't mean that they had to be friends—or do stuff together, to use his phrase. It didn't mean anything at all, right?

"Guess I'm the one," Harris admitted. There was a smile in his voice, just as there'd been two days ago on the beach. Fine; he could smile at Joey till his face fell off. "So is she around?" Harris wanted to know. "Maybe we can get started on that game of checkers she promised me."

I never promised you anything! Megan thought indignantly. Besides, where exactly did he think she'd go? This chair doesn't have sails or a propeller on it, she railed silently. It's not as if I could go tootling off around the island any old time I felt like it.

"She's in the kitchen helping Mom make cookies," Joey chirped happily, and Megan knew from the tone in his voice that he was thrilled to have company. "Chocolate chip," he added. "C'mon in; I bet they'll let you have some."

Arrrggghhh! Megan felt bands of panic squeeze her ribs. Maybe there was still time to race past the kitchen door, escape to the sanctuary of her bedroom on the porch, hide there until Harris gave up and went away—but before she could move, Joey had the door open and there was Harris, eyes still mild and blue behind his thick glasses, his legs as skinny and knobby-kneed as they'd been two days ago.

Joey pressed Harris into a kitchen chair. "It's him," he announced, as if Harris were an especially nice piece of flotsam he'd found washed up on the beach. "It's that guy you told us about, Megan. The one who wants you to play checkers."

Megan hoped there was a special place in Hades for little brothers like Joey. Her face felt so hot she was surprised it didn't burst into flames. She made a busy fuss about dusting flour off her hands, yet when she turned her wheelchair around she realized that her palms were greasy with sweat.

Seated across the table, Harris looked like a person whose palms never got greasy. "Hi, Megan," he said as easily as if they'd been meeting every summer like this for a million years.

"Uh, hi," she croaked, mortified by the sound of her own voice. "This is my mom, and that's"—Megan glared at Joey, who smiled back innocently—"that's my brother, Joey." Harris half rose from his chair and shook hands with each of them, causing Joey to grin as widely as a Halloween pumpkin. Then it was a done deed: Harris settled back in his chair, laid his checkerboard on the table, and helped himself to a chocolate chip cookie.

Joey attached himself to the edge of the table, only inches from where Harris sat. "You like to fish?" he asked, fixing Harris with an intent gaze. "Sometimes I go with my dad, but he only comes up weekends. Once in a while we get a walleye," he confided. "You ever catch a walleye?"

Harris dumped checker pieces onto the table and took a second cookie. "I cannot tell a lie, Joey," he said with mock gravity. "Not only have I never caught a walleye, I've never gone fishing in my entire life. Unless of course you want to count the time I changed the water in my goldfish bowl when I was eight and both my fish flopped out of the sink, forcing me to rescue the slimy little guys off the bathroom floor."

"Never gone fishing?" Joey echoed, shocked. He

leaned his chin in his hand and inspected Harris even more carefully. Soon a pleased expression crept across his narrow, sunburned face. Megan cringed. She was quite sure she knew exactly what Joey's next remark would be.

"I can show you how," Joey offered generously. "You can use Megan's pole."

Harris raised his eyebrows and glanced at her. "Red or black?" he asked.

"Neither one," Joey piped helpfully. "Her pole's green. Mine's blue. They're made out of fiberglass."

Harris winked at Megan, and his smile showed his rabbity front teeth, making him look peculiarly sweet. "I was asking your sister if she wanted to play on the red or the black, Joey," he explained, then waited for her answer.

"Um, red, I suppose," she heard herself mumble. Why did I say that, she wondered, especially when I haven't decided if I really want to play?

"About learning how to fish, Joey," Harris said, "maybe your sister would just as soon not lend her pole out to a total stranger."

"Doesn't matter," Megan snapped, "because I don't go fishing anymore." She spoke so loudly that both Mom and Joey turned to stare at her in amazement.

"Anyway, you said you were going to come over a couple of days ago," she reminded Harris, her voice still too loud. "How come you didn't?" Megan despised herself for asking, but suspicion, boiling deep inside, seemed to vomit the words out of her mouth. The question was so naked, so needy that she immediately felt worse, not better. Now he'd believe for sure that she'd actually cared if he showed up. Suddenly, Megan hated him. Joey too. Mom even, for standing there with that pained expression on her face. Herself most of all.

"Well, things over there"—Harris nodded in the direction of the Chambliss cottage—"got a little bit out of hand. Julia fell, see, so Andrew and I had to take her over to the mainland to the emergency drop-in center."

He called his mom and dad Julia and Andrew?

Mom pressed a floury hand over her heart. "Oh, my goodness!" she gasped. "I hope it wasn't anything serious. You ought to have let us know, Harris. Perhaps I could've—"

Harris studied the checkerboard in front of him. "Oh, that's okay," he murmured softly. "Julia has, well, a few bad days now and then."

"Bad days?" Mom frowned anxiously. "Is there anything I can do to help?" Mom, ever the patter and stroker of Persons in Need, Megan thought, and almost loved her mother again.

Harris shook his head. "No thanks; everything's okay now. It was just—just one of those things." He seemed determined not to pursue the topic of his mother's accident any further. He stacked the checkers into piles of red and black, then turned to Megan quizzically.

"So you really don't mind if I borrow your fishing pole?" he asked.

"No problem." Megan sighed. Suddenly, it wasn't.

Hearing that, Harris brightened. "Hey, why don't we all go together?" he suggested.

Megan stared at him. "Me? Go fishing?" A moment

ago she'd been willing to give him a second chance; he just blew that possibility away with his stupid idea. The truth was plain: He was just like everyone else who thought they knew what she ought to do better than she knew herself. A hot, resentful sensation coiled itself like a snake in Megan's chest.

"Want to know why these Velcro straps hold my feet in place on those footrests?" she demanded, narrowing her glance and pointing downward. "Because sometimes muscle spasms send my feet into the air like a pair of unguided missiles." Her voice was hard and bitter.

"Know why I have to drink gallons and gallons of cranberry juice? So that my pee will be acidic enough that I won't get another bladder infection. Know why I have to hoist myself up like this?" Megan paused in her tirade long enough to give Harris a demonstration. "So I won't get pressure sores on my rear end, that's why. And you think I ought to go *fishing*?"

But Joey brushed her words aside as if he hadn't heard a thing she'd said. "Gee, Megan, that sounds like a neat idea!" he exclaimed.

"Correction, Joey. It's a rotten one," Megan insisted. This time the loudness of her voice startled Rollie, who leaped to his feet and woofed softly, as if a stranger had just come into the cottage uninvited. "In case you haven't noticed," Megan said pointedly, tapping the arm of her chair, "I'm in a whee—"

"I noticed, Megan," Harris interrupted gently. "I just thought maybe there was a way we could figure out to—"

"Well, there isn't!" Megan blurted. She jerked her chair away from the table and raced toward her bedroom on the porch. She wished she could've left with a dramatic flourish, but flourishes were hard to manage when you were trapped in a chair. She let the porch door slam shut behind her. "And the only reason I said I'd play on the red is because it used to bring me luck!" she yelled over her shoulder. Luck? What a joke. It was something she'd never have again.

So let Bugs Bunny play checkers with Joey.

So let them go fishing together.

So let everyone quit trying to make decisions for her. Megan heard murmurings commence on the other side of the door. She didn't have to press her ear against it to know exactly what was being said.

She knew the story by heart, the Account of the Accident, the one Mom delivered to neighbors, relatives, her bridge club, all strangers who looked even faintly interested. It was as if everyone, Mom especially, thought Megan had lost her hearing along with the use of her legs.

Fifteen minutes later, Megan heard a faint, tuneless whistling beyond the porch windows. She glanced up to see Harris on his way back to the Chambliss cottage. His checkerboard was tucked under his arm. He paused after he vaulted onto the deck next door and stopped whistling. He brushed cookie crumbs off his shirt. He turned to stare across the lake, looking lonesome and lost.

*I did it again*, Megan realized.

The hot, bitter lump in her chest turned into a loose knot of regret. It wouldn't have killed her to have played a game of checkers with the poor guy. Or when he made that suggestion about going fishing, she could have refused with a smile and said, "Not today, Harris. Maybe some other time." Instead, she'd gotten into one of her famous snits, had been a jerk—again.

No wonder Bev quit coming to the hospital; Megan remembered how she'd avoided looking at Bev, had refused to talk to her beyond a monosyllable or two, had made herself unavailable. The truth was, Bev had tried to be a friend. It wasn't that Bev was afraid of getting close to that hospital bed Megan realized, it was that she didn't want her to.

What Harris didn't know—and maybe Mom and Dad and Joey didn't know it, either—was that part of her wanted to act like the old Megan, but the new Megan wouldn't allow it. After the accident, it had been too hard to tell the difference between friendship and pity, and although she wanted the first so badly she ached inside, she hated the second so much she'd never permit herself to take a chance.

"I figured I'd be doing a Robinson Crusoe shtick all summer," Harris said two days ago on the beach. Recalling those words, Megan tried to imagine what the summer was like for *him*. Not a picnic, probably, having parents who must be a lot older than most kids' folks. Next door, the draperies were never opened; no sounds of summer nonsense issued from the Chambliss cottage as it had during other vacations. Playing checkers or going fishing or having a barbecue at night on the beach were things Julia and Andrew apparently never did.

Megan lightly stroked her denim-covered knees as she watched Harris disappear into the cottage next door. Okay, Megan she told herself, tomorrow *you're* the one who's going to get real. This is serious, so pay attention. Tomorrow, you'll go over there—wheelchair and all—and you'll apologize. "Look, Harris," you'll say, "sorry about yesterday. I was a jerk. You still want to play checkers?"

No more weaseling out of stuff, Megan decided. Hey, there were worse things to do with a summer than try to be somebody's Friday, right?

Megan woke, roused out of a sound sleep.

She pulled the medicine cart closer and peered at the clock. Two A.M. There was no moon nor any stars out, so the porch was as black as a cave. No wind rustled the leaves beyond the windows; all was drenched in silence. It was quite easy to hear the sound of someone weeping on the deck next door.

"You're making too much out of it," a man said in a low, urgent voice. It must be Andrew, Harris's father. "Just because the offers don't come in as fast and furious as they used to doesn't mean the whole world's forgotten about you, Julia," he went on. "You've just had a dry spell, that's all. It could happen to even the most famous actress. Why, when we get home, I'll bet—"

"When we get home it'll be the same old thing—wait, wait, wait for the calls that never come!" a woman interrupted tearfully. "No telegrams, no messages on the answering machine, no mail in the mailbox!" Julia, Harris's mom, probably. Next came a noisy honking into a tissue, then a heavy sigh of resignation.

"I suppose I made a mistake when I turned down the part of Annie in *When Morning Comes*," Julia went on. "But I just couldn't see myself playing the part of an old hag before I really am one, Daddy!" In the dark, Megan opened her eyes wide. Harris called his parents by their first names but his mother called her husband Daddy?

"Ah, Julia, don't say that," Andrew protested in a low, soothing voice. "You'll never be an old hag, not to me, not to anyone who loves you. Getting older doesn't mean you can't act circles around performers twice and three times as young—and you've got a closetful of awards to prove it, too!" More weeping followed, then added assurances, all too soft to be heard in detail, and next came muffled footfalls, the closing of a door, and all was silent again.

Megan lay wide awake in the velvety summer blackness. On the beach that first morning Harris had said his last name was St. John . . . his mother's name apparently was Julia . . . from the sound of it, she must be an actress . . . was it possible, then, that she was Julia St. John? *The* Julia St. John? Mom had been crazy about her movies forever and must've watched *Return to Amberlee* at least a dozen times on the VCR back home.

Megan couldn't hold back a smile. Mom would be so thrilled; it'd be a hundred times better than having Sallie

Chambliss and all her crazy recipes next door! In the morning, at breakfast, she'd lay the big news on Mom and Joey.

"You'll never guess who Harris's mother is," she'd announce, then would make them try, knowing they'd never come up with the right answer in a million years. "Julia St. John, that's who," she'd finally tell them, "and according to what I heard last night, she thinks she's turning into an old hag."

**7**

"Meggie, you don't mean it!" Mom exclaimed at breakfast, and clasped her hands under her chin, her eyes bright with astonishment. "Julia St. John is living right next door? For the whole summer, you said?"

Megan couldn't hold back a grin. "I'm pretty sure it's her, all right," she assured her mother. It felt great to be the bearer of good news for a change. "And I don't think she's a very happy camper, if any of the stuff I heard last night is true," she added.

Mom's hands flew from beneath her chin like a pair of birds in flight. "I'd planned to invite them over just because it's the neighborly thing to do, but now it'll be kind of scary!" she chattered nervously. "I mean— Julia St. John! Here I am without any of my nice dishware from home or my good tablecloths, and no doubt she's used to nothing but the best! She's probably stayed in the nicest hotels everywhere, traveled all over the world, and she'll expect—"

"It's summertime, Mom, and this is Michigan," Megan pointed out. "Julia St. John must be on vacation, too; she won't expect anything too ritzy. If she'd wanted that, she'd have opted to go some place a lot fancier than Frenchman's Island. Maybe she just wants to be a regular person for a change and eat off paper plates like everyone else."

Mom hooked a pinkie in the corner of her mouth and nibbled it thoughtfully. "How do you think I ought to invite them over?" she mused. "I mean, should I send a little handwritten note over with Joey? Or would it be better to call her on the phone? Ummm . . . maybe the note would be best; it's most likely what she's accustomed to. It would give her time to decide if she really wants to meet us or not."

"Sounds good to me," Megan agreed. "Write it up, and I'll go over this morning."

"You?" Mom echoed, halting her coffee cup midway to her lips. Joey's jaw dropped, and milk trickled out of the left side of his mouth. A moment later, Mom's glance softened and a that's-my-old-Meggie expression warmed her eyes. Wisely, however, she didn't put her sentiment into words.

"I planned to go over there anyway to apologize to Harris," Megan explained. "Let's face it, I was sort of a dork yesterday."

Mom nodded slightly, but the admission made Joey bob his head six times in agreement. "The poor kid left here looking like somebody'd beaned him with a fry pan," Mom agreed. "I suppose he'd really been looking

59

forward to spending time with someone closer to his own age. Having parents who are so much older probably has made growing up a rather different experience for him."

"You make Julia St. John sound ancient," Megan observed, "which I guess is exactly what's been on her mind lately, judging from how she carried on last night."

"Ummm, I'd guess she must be past fifty," Mom replied. "I'll bet she doesn't look it, though. Nowadays, plastic surgery and tummy tucks can keep movie stars looking young forever. And Mr. Hassler must've been wrong about her hair; it's probably a very pretty shade of red, just like it is in her movies, not the color of iodine at all."

"Well, as soon as you get your invitation written out, I'll take it over," Megan repeated matter-of-factly.

"But you can't," Joey objected around a mouthful of toast. His eyes were round with disbelief. "Mom better give it to me. I'll do it."

"No problem," Megan insisted. "I *can* do it."

Mom and Joey both studied her with a mixture of doubt and sympathy. "How?" Joey demanded finally.

"I'll use that path out back that we always took to go into the woods, remember?" Megan reminded them. It commenced at the stoop of the back door to the cottage, was barely wide enough to accommodate a wheelchair, and had been worn as smooth and hard as concrete by many summers of use. The news made Joey look so disappointed that Megan decided she'd better offer him a consolation.

"Listen, Joey, when I'm over there I'll ask Harris if

he wants to go fishing with you, okay?'' Joey allowed that that might make him feel better, but although Megan waited all morning for the draperies to be pulled away from the windows next door, by noontime they still hadn't been.

Finally, after the lunch dishes were done, Megan wheeled herself to the back door, unwilling to wait any longer for a sign of life at the Chambliss cottage, and found herself face-to-face with the shadowy woods that loomed behind both cottages. Their own cottage had been built so snugly against the hillside that the stoop was nearly level with the ground. She'd be able to wheel herself off it quite easily, Megan realized, but would probably have to ask Mom and Joey for help getting back on it when she returned.

The wheelchair thunked heavily onto the path. Rolling along, surrounded by the trees and vines of the island that once had been so familiar, Megan felt another one of those pangs of loss that the rehab counselors had warned her about. Until this moment, she'd either hardened herself against the pain that such loss always brought or had given into it and turned to mush inside.

Today, somehow, its impact was different.

So what if once you flew along this trail like a woodland sprite? she asked herself. Now the sprite's got wheels—no reason to ruin everything that's left of your life. Anyway, some things hadn't changed at all. Look over there, she told herself, as if she'd become her own counselor. Beneath a tree was a thick carpet of prince's pine. Megan took a deep sniff of the fragrance of the delicate pink, bell-shaped flowers that filled the air. No matter what had happened, flowers still smelled sweet, her counselor-self reminded her.

As she wheeled slowly toward the Chambliss cottage, a pair of red squirrels fled from the path and chittered up a nearby poplar, where they scolded her from a branch a few feet over her head. In the blue sky beyond them, she could see a red-tailed hawk coast lazily on the air currents above the island. So much of what she'd always loved about Frenchman's Island was still here—a shadowy path, a pair of sassy squirrels, a lone hawk. Maybe I would've realized this sooner, Megan admitted privately, if I hadn't spent all my time sulking on the porch.

A moment later, however, her philosophical ruminations were challenged by a real-life dilemma. She'd forgotten that the cottage next door was built on a much shallower slope of the hillside and that its stoop was a full two steps off the ground. She wouldn't be able to get any closer to the back door of the Chambliss cottage than about six feet from it. No way could she reach out to knock on it.

Megan fiddled with the note in her pocket. She debated about calling Harris's name. No; that would be too much like a little kid going next door to call for a playmate to come out. Instead, she set the brakes on her chair, then leaned over to pick up several small pebbles from the edge of the path. One by one, she pitched them lightly against the back door of the Chambliss cottage, hoping that someone inside—preferably Julia St. John rather than her son Harris—would hear.

*Plonk. Plink. Plonk.* No one opened the back door.

One more try, Megan decided. *Plonk. Plink. Plonk.*

When the door finally flew open, she was so startled she flattened herself against the back of her chair and stared, openmouthed.

The woman who swayed in the doorway like a tree in a strong breeze looked much older than fifty. Mascara and eyeshadow had seeped into the creases around her eyes, giving her a haggard expression. There was a dark bruise on her left cheek, perhaps from the fall Harris said she'd taken. Her mouth was a brilliant scarlet slash that resembled an injury more than it did a fashion statement. And Mr. Hassler was right after all: Her hair *was* the color of iodine and hung in tattered ribbons around her pale, ravaged face.

Julia St. John had said she didn't want to play old hags before she really was one, but it was plain to Megan that the dreaded metamorphosis was already in full progress.

"Hoor you?" the actress demanded in a thick, blurred voice. She waved a long-stemmed glass in Megan's direction. It was half-full of amber liquid. Probably not mouthwash, Megan decided.

"I—I—I wonder if—that is, my mother would like to—to—to invite you—"

"Don't mumble, girl, speak up!" Julia St. John ordered imperiously. "I can't understand a word yoor saying!"

Suddenly, Harris materialized out of the gloom behind his mother. "It's Megan, Julia," he explained gently. "I told you about her, remember? She's the girl who's staying in the cottage next door."

"Wha's she want?" Julia asked crossly. "And wha's

*that*?'' she demanded, pointing indignantly at the wheelchair. "It looks like—like—a *wheel*chair!" The word was uttered with something akin to disgust, as if the sight of such an object were an affront to her delicate sensibilities.

"It *is* a wheelchair, Julia. Remember, I told you about the accident Megan had.''

"Accident? *I'm* the one who fell and had to go to the emergency room!" Julia insisted peevishly. "But what did I expect," she ranted on, "coming to such a godforsaken place! I must've been crazy to let you and Andrew talk me into coming here for the whole summer!" Expending energy for a tantrum seemed to exhaust her, for the actress abruptly reeled away from the door and with a dismissive wave of her hand vanished inside the cottage.

Megan wished there were someplace to look except straight at Harris. He must feel terribly embarrassed to have his mother carry on so badly. She was surprised, then, to see a wry smile on his lips. "Julia's having another bad day,'' he said with a sigh, lifting both shoulders philosophically.

"Does she have . . . umm . . . lots of them?" Megan inquired discreetly, wondering how many of Julia St. John's bad days had something to do with the fact that it probably wasn't Listerine in that glass.

Harris nodded. "Bad days—and weeks—and sometimes months. These last few years haven't been so great for my grandmother.''

"Your—*grand*mother?" Megan regretted she wasn't able to disguise her disbelief. "But my mother—we all—everybody figured she was your mom!"

"In a way that's what Julia's been," Harris acknowledged. "My parents died a long time ago. My dad was Julia's only son. I've lived with her—and whoever she was married to—since I was just a little kid."

"So, like, you mean she's been married before?"

"Lots of befores. About five of them, to be exact."

"I guess Andrew isn't your grandfather, then?"

"Nope. Andrew is Andrew. He's a good guy, though, and he tries hard to make Julia happy, which lately has become a full-time career for both him and me."

"I'm sorry," Megan offered clumsily. *Sorry* seemed like a wimp word when you'd just discovered someone was an orphan, that he'd lived most of his life with a lady who apparently got married often and got her jollies from a bottle. "Anyway, what I came over about is my mom wants your folks—your grandparents, I mean—to come over this weekend when my dad gets up from the city." She held out Mom's carefully printed invitation.

Harris accepted the piece of blue, folded paper. "I think Julia would like that; it'll be something to look forward to. I'll give it to her tomorrow."

"And—" Megan felt herself color up. "I've got a couple of invitations just for you. Joey wants like mad to teach you how to fish. All you need to do to make my brother happy is just pretend you're interested. And I—" The next part wasn't quite as easy to put into words. "I mean, if you still want to play that game of checkers, I'll play on the black just to give you a break."

"Thanks," Harris responded. Knowing what she now knew, Megan decided that he looked different. Older, somehow, than when he'd been in the kitchen eating cookies. Losing his parents when he was just a kid, then living with Julia and all her husbands must have made him grow up in a hurry.

As if he were able to read her thoughts, Harris cautioned, "Don't think too badly of my grandmother." He shoved his fists into the pockets of his shorts and rocked back and forth on his heels. "You've gotta understand that Julia's an actress. She thinks that getting old is practically worse than dying. Her problem, see, is she can't stand the person she's turned into."

*Can't stand the person she's turned into . . .*

But that's *my* problem! Megan objected silently, as if she owned it. Julia St. John has been rich and famous and has been married lots of times, but those are things that'll never happen to me. That old lady ought to think about how lucky she'd been instead of feeling so sorry for herself.

Discreetly, Megan raised herself off the seat of her chair, then lowered herself back down. "I don't think your grandmother's got too much to complain about," she observed with a pinched smile. "I could write the book on what it means to turn into someone you never intended to be."

"You mean—?" Harris pointed at her wheelchair and let his question hang in the air.

"Exactly." Megan sighed. "I heard my mom telling you all about the accident, so I won't bore you with further details."

Not that she would've been able to, because at that moment Joey came flying down the path. "You've been gone so long, Megan!'' he cried. ''Me and Mom got worried so I—'' He stopped dead in his tracks when he spied Harris. ''Yo, Harris!'' he hailed. ''I got the poles all ready. Got some good bait, too, worms I dug myself. Afternoon's a good time of day to fish, so if you want to—''

''If you say it's a good time to fish, then let's fish,'' Harris agreed, and hopped off the Chambliss back stoop. As he ran past her chair, Megan felt his fingertips skip a light tattoo across her shoulder. ''See ya later for that game,'' he promised. ''Right now I've got to learn how to lure the wily walleye onto my hook or into a net or whatever.''

Megan caught his wrist. ''Wait,'' she whispered.

Harris paused, surprised. ''What did you throw into the lake that night I saw you on the end of the dock?'' Megan asked. Before the summer got an hour older, she needed to know if he had a girlfriend.

Harris flushed. ''Rocks,'' he confessed. ''Little ones.''

''Little rocks?''

''Yeah. I made wishes on them.''

''Wishes?''

''Yeah. That maybe this would be the summer Julia would get outside of herself. Think about Andrew—and me—and the rest of her life for a change. Things have been hard for her lately, but she doesn't realize they've been hard for us too.'' Then he vanished down the path behind Joey. Megan watched him and stroked her unfeeling knees. It didn't matter, not really truly, but she was sort of relieved that he hadn't said he'd broken up with someone named Monica and was hoping they'd get back together.

By the time she got back to the cottage, she could see around its corner that Joey and Harris were climbing into the *Dolly*. It was plain that Harris didn't know much more about boats than he did about fishing because he nearly fell in the lake twice as he tried to get on board.

Joey, of course, was only too pleased to take over completely, Megan saw, and as soon as they shoved off from the dock he handed an oar to Harris and showed him how to use it. Harris began to stir the water as if he were stirring soup, then glanced up to see her watching.

"Maybe next time you'll come with us," he called, waving.

Megan waved back. "Maybe I will," she answered, softly enough so that he wouldn't quite be able to hear. "Maybe I will." Starting over . . . picking up the pieces . . . getting used to losing the old Megan and living with the new one. . . . Did she have the nerve to take a chance on stuff like that? Megan took a deep breath. Well, if I keep trying maybe I can find a way to do it before summer is over, she decided. Maybe I can.

**8**

The pink, plastic serving tray with its load of appetizers was as pretty as Mom could make tuna fish on crackers look. Joey had sliced stuffed olives in half and put two on each canapé, where they ogled passersby like pairs of green eyes with red pupils. Megan made tiny cheese-balls, rolled them in chopped walnuts, and skewered each on a colored toothpick.

"But of course this can't hold a candle to what Julia St. John probably expects," Mom lamented as she whisked a dustcloth across the porch furniture and plumped up the worn sofa pillows. Dad had tried to help by picking daisies and stuffing them in a large, blue bowl, where they now decorated the coffee table.

"And don't I wish I'd remembered to bring my long summer skirt to wear," Mom fretted. "This outfit doesn't seem quite—" She plucked unhappily at her faded chambray skirt and hot pink T-shirt with its purple announcement, NO. 1 MOM.

"You look just like you always do," Joey assured her.

"That's exactly what I'm afraid of," Mom groaned.

"Megan's right, sweetie," Dad soothed. "It's vacation time; the fabulous Julia St. John will just have to rough it like the rest of us peasants. If it's been good enough for the Murphys for fourteen summers, I'm sure it won't be the death of her for one."

As Megan listened, she studied her legs critically. For half an hour every afternoon she'd worked on tanning them, and now they were a pleasing shade of coffee-with-cream. In shorts, with tennies and ankle socks, she hoped that she looked almost like an ordinary teenager who was in a wheelchair only temporarily with, say, a broken ankle. With luck, the sight of the chair wouldn't upset the actress as much as it had a few days ago.

Before anyone could agonize further about tuna fish, faded skirts, or wheelchairs, the new neighbors were at the door. Andrew rapped lightly, and when Dad opened the screen, Julia swept into the room like a queen headed for her coronation.

For Mom's sake, Megan was glad to see that Julia looked much better than when she'd stood in the doorway of the Chambliss cottage three days ago. Her violently red hair was wrapped around her head like a turban, and enormous gold hoops hung from her ears. The outfit she wore reminded Megan of a harem girl's, with its ballooning pant legs and fringed sash that hung to her knees. Every finger on each of the actress's hands was decorated with a ring, and gold bangles and brace-

70

lets went halfway up each arm. She seemed to fill up the room with her presence, and Joey, hunched on the sofa beside Rollie, stared at her with astonishment.

"Weren't you darlings to invite us over!" Julia purred in a voice as rich and smooth as butterscotch syrup. Today, Megan noticed, her words weren't blurred. Harris came through the door last. "Hi, Murphys," he greeted everyone, and gave Joey a pair of high fives.

"Little did I ever dream that someday my grandson would be my entrée to high society," Julia teased huskily. The moment her gaze settled on the wheelchair, however, Megan saw the actress glance quickly aside. I guess shorts and tanned legs aren't going to do it, she realized. Trouble is, Julia can't see *me*; she can only see my chair.

Dad had a tray ready with tall, frosted glasses of lemonade. Julia stared at them, amazed. "It's lemonade," Dad explained as he held the tray for her inspection. "We added fresh mint that Joey and I gathered in the woods this morning before the sun was up."

"Lemonade?" Julia echoed. What had she expected? Megan wondered. Martinis? Mouthwash? The actress gingerly selected a glass from the tray and stared down into it. "My, it's been years and *years* since I had a glass of lemonade!" she murmured, struggling to hide her disappointment.

"You don't know how thrilled I am to meet you," Mom bubbled, and seemed to have forgotten that she was dressed like someone on vacation. "I think I saw *Return to Amberlee* at least a dozen times; you were

71

wonderful in it!'' Mom looked even younger and prettier than usual, Megan observed, and saw Julia's green eyes grow narrow with alarm.

Was it Mom's smooth, flushed face, the lemonade, or the compliment that most unnerved Julia? Megan wondered. ''Oh, my, I made that film such a long, long time ago,'' the actress whispered vaguely, and gulped her lemonade as if she wished to block out any recollection of how the years had passed since the movie had gotten several Academy Awards, including one for best actress. ''I'll never be that good or that young again.'' She sighed.

In the corner of the living room, Dad engaged Andrew in a conversation about the investment firm of Dorsey and Matchlock, while Harris stood quietly nearby. Then Megan overheard Mom issue another invitation to Julia.

''If you aren't doing anything next Wednesday, J-J-J-Julia''—she had a hard time calling her former idol by her first name, Megan noticed—''maybe you'd like to go with us to the mainland to the summer craft fair. It's really lots of fun, and I often find whimsical little gifts to use as stocking stuffers at Christmastime. We could all take the ferry over on Wednesday morning and be back here by suppertime.''

The idea of going to a craft fair seemed to shock the actress as much as the sight of fresh lemonade had. Then the hard look in Julia's emerald eyes softened, and she laid a jeweled hand on Mom's arm. ''Why, how sweet of you to suggest it, dear. Ummm, yes, I suppose such a venture might be, ah, rather amusing.''

''Oh, you'll have lots of fun,'' Joey assured her. ''I

always do. They've got cotton candy and foot-long hot dogs and everything. No Ferris wheel or Tilt-a-Whirl, though. It isn't exactly that kind of fair.''

"How . . . how . . . quaint," Julia murmured, studying Joey as if she'd quite forgotten what a nine-year-old person looked like.

When the threesome departed two hours later, they left as they'd arrived: Julia led the way with a flourish of fabric, bangles, and scarlet hair, leaving the room curiously empty and dull. When they were gone, Megan realized she'd said only two words to poor Harris the whole afternoon, "Hi" and "Bye."

"She's certainly much different than I thought she'd be," Mom admitted as soon as she was sure the trio was behind closed doors in the neighboring cottage.

"She's a lot older, for one thing," Dad noted. "Unless I miss my guess, she's chasing sixty down the road with a stick."

"Nowadays that doesn't have to mean *old*," Mom objected warmly. "But you know, I can't help feeling a bit sorry for her. Imagine—me feeling sorry for Julia St. John! But she seemed rather, well, sort of lonely."

"I don't know about lonely," Joey put in, "but I think she'd look a lot better if she didn't put so much goop on her face. You guys see those eyelashes? One of 'em was coming unglued! If you found it on the floor, you'd think it was a caterpillar and you'd stick it in a jar!"

"Shush," Mom hushed with a smile. "Julia wears a lot of makeup because she's accustomed to being on

73

stage or in front of a camera. Eyelashes and goop are part of her trade, Joey, like jeans and tennies are part of mine.''

Megan let their conversation about Julia wash around her like warm lake water. She knew only one thing for sure: Before next Wednesday rolled around, she'd have to figure out a way to get out of going to the craft fair with the rest of them.

The prospect of wheeling herself past booths filled with handmade baskets, dried flower arrangements, and crocheted pot holders while the summer sun scalded the back of her neck was not inviting. Nor was the challenge of getting into and out of overcrowded rest rooms one she intended to subject herself to.

How to put the decision to Mom was another matter. Megan decided that the best thing to do would be to make it seem as if it'd be a big inconvenience to Julia. Timing would be important, too. I'll wait until Wednesday morning, she schemed. It'll be too late then for Mom to raise a fuss; she'll let me off the hook rather than make a scene in front of her heroine.

By Wednesday, Megan had perfected a speech. "It'll annoy her a bunch, Mom," she pointed out. "Julia St. John is used to being the one who's waited on, not to having to wait on somebody else. If I go along, you know for sure that's what'll happen. Besides, I think my wheelchair bothers her; she avoids looking at me as if I were a leper or something. Anyway, I'll be fine right here. Rollie can keep me company, and I'll have supper ready for you guys when you get back.''

Megan braced herself for Mom's declaration of "Absolutely not!" or "Out of the question!" and was relieved when she didn't trash the idea right away.

"Golly, Megan, are you sure you don't want to come? We could manage somehow, and it might be good for Julia to think about someone other than her own wonderful self for a change. On the other hand, if you really don't—"

"I really don't," Megan said quickly, before Mom had a chance to have second thoughts. Then Mom's frown turned into a pleased smile.

"Say, I'll bet Harris would agree to stay with you if you asked him," Mom suggested as if it were the best idea since sliced bread.

"Forget it!" Joey yelped. "I want Harris to come with us!"

"Harris isn't a member of the Baby-Sitter's Club, Mom," Megan groaned. "You're not thinking about what *he* might like; you're thinking about what would make *you* more comfortable. Well, don't."

"Yeah, don't," Joey chimed in eagerly.

"Be reasonable, Megan," Mom urged. "We'll be gone at least six or eight hours, and I won't really be able to have a good time if I'm thinking about you being here by yourself all that time."

"Get that dorky Billy Pritchard and his dumb sister to come over and keep Megan company," Joey suggested.

"All right already," Megan groaned. "Ask Harris. Just don't expect *me* to ask him." It was hard to imagine how such a conversation might go:

"By the way, Harris, my mom would like you to baby-sit."

"Oh, sure, no problem. Joey's a neat little guy."

"No, Harris. Not for Joey."

"Not for Joey?"

"No."

"Who for?"

"Me."

Help! The idea was so humiliating, and what was worse, Harris would be embarrassed, too.

But when he trotted up the ramp five minutes after the ferry left, Harris didn't seem embarrassed in the slightest. "Whew!" he exclaimed, and wiped his hand across his forehead in mock relief. "Saved in the nick of time. No way did I want to go to a craft fair, whatever that is. The last time I went to a fair I barfed my hot dog halfway through my ride on the Serpent. Nathan wasn't especially thrilled with me, as I recall."

"Nathan?"

"Nathan Medvig. He was Julia's third husband. When she was doing *The Glass Menagerie* in summer stock one season—a gig between movies, y'know—sometimes he'd take me to Coney Island if she had a matinee."

"I used to love fairs," Megan said, and sighed, relieved that they weren't going to have to discuss baby-sitting per se. "My favorite one was the county fair near the town where we live. It's in August, the week before school starts. That's where everybody from Hudson High gets together for the first time since school let out in June. It was neat to hear what everyone's been doing. I went last year. That was only a couple of months before—''

The silence that fell between them was awkward. ''Before the accident?'' Harris finished for her. Megan nodded.

''I suppose getting used to what happened is as hard for you as getting old is for my grandmother,'' he observed softly.

''No lie,'' Megan heard herself agree. It felt good to be able to talk about such things to someone her own age. It had been too hard to say anything to Bev, and Dex had never come by, perhaps because he was afraid of what he might hear. ''And Julia's not going to get over her problem any quicker than I'm going to get over mine,'' she added with a wry smile, tapping the arm of her wheelchair. The words sounded grim but funny too, and they both started to laugh.

''So anyway, what's a baby-sitter supposed to do?'' Harris wanted to know. ''I never sat a baby before, not to mention a person who's practically grown.''

Megan surprised herself by laughing again. ''Don't sweat it; I don't need watching. The main reason you're here is to make my mom happy, or in case something bad happens again, like Rollie finding another broken Pepsi bottle somewhere.''

''Maybe we ought to play that game of checkers we're always talking about,'' Harris suggested, turning to peer through the kitchen screen at the beach below. ''Or hey, we could take the boat out.''

"Take the boat out?" Megan repeated, startled.

"Sure. We could, you know, fix ourselves sort of a picnic lunch and just row around out there in the bay for a while."

Megan wheeled herself to the kitchen door and peered out, too. Joey had left the *Dolly* tied to the end of the dock; its name, printed on its yellow side in large, black, cartoon-style letters, showed just above the waterline. "I don't think there's any way I could ever get into it," she objected quietly.

"I could help you," Harris offered. "Want to give it a try?"

*Want to give it a try . . . ?*

The question was short and simple but implied risks and challenges. It was huge, like the word *forever,* and Megan couldn't quite take hold of it. What if I goof up? she agonized silently. Well, so what if you do? her braver self replied. The only one who'd see was Harris, a guy she'd probably never see again after this summer. It wasn't as if she'd meet him in the halls at Hudson or anyplace else; after this summer their paths would not likely cross again. In a way, Harris didn't matter. What *did* matter was that he'd invited her to try on a piece of real life to see if it was the right size.

"Yeah," Megan answered slowly. "I think maybe I do."

# 9

"I guess I forgot to mention that helping me wouldn't be easy," Megan groaned as she wiped the sweat out of her eyes.

It was the third time Harris had waded out to the *Dolly* with her in his arms and had tried to lift her into it. Each time he approached the boat, however, it floated just out of reach, as skittish as a pony, making a transfer impossible.

Megan kept both arms locked around his neck as tight as a noose as Harris staggered up the beach and lowered her back into her wheelchair. She glanced up apologetically, noticing that his face was pale and shiny with perspiration, that his knees were quivery from the exertion of the three futile attempts they'd made.

Harris braced his fists against his hips and squinted at the yellow boat bobbing on the blue water. "Hey, did you ever ride piggyback when you were a little kid?" he demanded suddenly.

"I suppose so," Megan muttered, "but I don't see what that has to do with anything."

"What I was thinking," Harris went on, "was that maybe I could haul you out there on my back."

"On your back?" Megan echoed, frowning. "I don't see how that would work any better than what we just tried to—"

"Trust me," Harris assured her, growing more enthused about his plan. "See, if I had you on my back I could keep one hand free, and then when I edged up alongside the *Dolly* I could hold her steady, and you could just sort of—"

"Yeah, right, topple into her on my head," Megan finished, "or worse yet, get dumped into the lake where I'd sink like a rock and probably drown. Some babysitter you turned out to be!" The whole thing was so hopeless that she giggled to keep from crying with frustration.

"No, really, I think it might work," Harris insisted. "It'd sure help, though, if there was some way you could slide off my back, then safely down into the bottom of the boat."

"Wait—I've got a transfer board!" Megan exclaimed, beginning to see possibilities in his scheme. "It's on the medicine cart next to my bed. Why don't you run back to the cottage and get it?"

In a moment, Harris returned with the transfer board under his arm, plus her pillow and the red-plaid blanket from the end of her bed. "Wow, talk about high-tech innovations, huh?" he joked. He waded out to the *Dolly*, laid the folded blanket and the pillow in the bottom of the boat, and leaned the board slantwise against them. He hurried back to where Megan waited, turned his back to her, and dropped to his knees in the sand in front of her chair.

"What're you doing now?" she demanded, puzzled.

"Lean forward so you can wrap your arms around my neck," Harris ordered.

"Listen, Harris, I'm not so sure—"

"It'll work, it'll work," he promised, and, peering over his shoulder, inched backward to position himself even closer to her chair. "For starters, brace yourself with your hands against my shoulders, okay?"

Megan, surprised to find herself doing so, leaned forward. Beneath her palms, Harris's shoulders were as hard and bony as his knees looked. "Now what?" she asked through clenched teeth. But it was too late for questions: She'd already lost her balance and could feel herself pitching forward. She collapsed helplessly against Harris's backbone like a sack of flour dumped off a truck.

But instead of letting her fall onto the sand, Harris reached back and hooked an arm under each of her knees. With a grunt, he staggered to his feet, made his way down the beach as carefully as if he were walking on eggshells, then waded slowly out to the *Dolly*.

"I'll have to let go of your right knee," he warned when he sidled up to the boat, "so I can hold 'er steady." Megan glanced down in time to see her leg slip along Harris's hip and dangle uselessly in the blue water.

*So odd*. She'd never get used to it: the knowledge that the water was cool, wet, refreshing, yet she felt no sensation whatever. Was it possible that a person never accepted the fact that what had been lost was truly lost . . . ?

"Are you lined up with the side of the boat?" Harris wanted to know. "Close enough so your tush is next to that transfer board?"

Megan eyed the boat. "Pull the *Dolly* over a little bit more," she urged, "and hold her as steady as you can." This is why I never went back to Hudson, she realized. Everything that had been so easy became so hard. All the clumsiness, all the effort it took to figure out new ways to do old things. Once, she just hauled off and climbed into the *Dolly*, for heaven's sake! Now it was something that had to be plotted and schemed and programmed. It was just too—

"This isn't going to work, Harris," she hissed in his ear. "Let's just forget it, okay? Maybe we'd better go back and play that game of checkers after all."

But the words were scarcely out of her mouth before she felt herself falling again, as she'd fallen against his backbone moments earlier. Seconds later she found herself sprawled ingloriously on the pillow and blanket at the bottom of the boat. Her once-upon-a-time-gorgeous, suntanned legs stuck out in front of her, each foot cocked at a different angle, like a rag doll's.

"See, we did it!" Harris exclaimed gleefully, and gave her shoulder a congratulatory pat. He hoisted himself, wet and dripping, into the boat and began to fumble with the oars.

Megan righted herself on the pile of blankets, reached down to rearrange her legs, then leaned against the boat seat behind her. "The oars fit into those gizmos," she gasped, pointing at the oarlocks.

"Aye, aye, sir," Harris obeyed, and gave her a delighted, rabbity smile. She hadn't noticed before, but even with those dumb little glasses and that skinny frame he was almost cute. Not to-die-for-California cute, like Dex Cooper, but down-to-earth-and-comfy cute, like your best friend's cousin from out of town might be.

Harris began to row in wide, lazy circles a few feet from shore, always in view of the cottages. Then he craned his neck and nodded over his shoulder. "What's out there?" he wanted to know, gesturing toward the blob of green in the distance that seemed to float as insubstantially as a leaf on the mild, blue water.

Megan didn't answer right away. *Paradise*, she was tempted to tell him. What you're looking at, my friend, is what once was paradise to me.

"Joey and I called it the Hideout," she answered casually, as if it were no place special. It was hard to realize that it was a place she'd probably never see again close up, would only see as she did now, from a distance.

"It's just a little bitty thing," she explained, "a couple of blocks long, a block wide, hardly deserves to be called an island at all. Not much more than an outcropping of sand and trees and rock, actually. I used to row out there once in a while." Once in a while? Hardly; she used to go out there nearly every morning all summer long, just to watch the sun come up.

"Want to go out there now?" Harris asked.

Megan stared at him, astonished and speechless. No kidding, this guy had a genuine talent for coming up with preposterous ideas as if they were the most ordinary things in the world. She looked past him at the Hideout. "Out there?" she repeated in a small voice. What would it be like to lie on that dear, tiny beach again, to let the water, blue as lapis lazuli under the June sun, wash across her toes—even if her toes couldn't feel it anymore?

Megan turned her gaze away, toward the safety of the cottages. "We'd better not," she murmured vaguely. She trailed her fingers in the water and made a quick mental inventory of what she'd tossed into the canvas bag she'd packed before they got into the *Dolly*: lotion, tissues, a sweatshirt, matches, some stuff to eat. She studied the beckoning spot of green floating on the horizon.

"Well, why not?" she blurted. She smiled with a bravery she only partly felt. "Row away, matey!" she urged, before she could chicken out.

The first time she and Joey went to the Hideout together, he was only five; he was too little yet to row, so she'd done it all herself. She was only eleven, and how her arms had ached! Later, when he got bigger, it was easier to make the trip because Joey liked to help. Now, seeing how flushed Harris was, Megan knew exactly how he felt. A mustache of sweat gleamed on his upper lip, and a triangle of perspiration hung like a dark shield across his T-shirted chest.

"Wish I could help you out," she murmured.

"Who said you can't?" Harris challenged, panting.

"Well, I—" Jeez, wasn't it perfectly obvious why she couldn't? Once again, Harris seemed like an obtuse dummy, a dork, to use Joey's favorite word. A moment ago, she'd decided he was sort of a dish; now he didn't seem cute at all. "I just *can't*, that's all!" Megan insisted.

"I bet you've got muscles you can't even count," Harris groaned. "Wheeling that chair all the time must be great exercise. You're probably in ten times better shape than I am. I'm a city kid, remember? Most summers my main athletic event is to walk down to Sam's Deli on Forty-Seventh Street to get a pastrami on rye with a garlic pickle on the side."

"But rowing would be just too—" Megan tried to object.

"How will you know until you try?" Harris countered. "I bet if you got up on that seat behind you and balanced yourself with the oars you could row practically as well as I can."

The boat seat he referred to pressed against Megan's shoulder blades, making it impossible to ignore his suggestion. It shocked her to think he might be right. What if she could row the *Dolly* as she'd rowed it in the old days?

Megan half turned on her cushion and attempted to hoist herself onto the wooden seat. No way. It'd take a wholehearted effort, not any delicate, sissy maneuver. She twisted herself around so that she hung over the seat and tried not to think what she must look like from behind. In the hot sun it was exhausting work to pull up, up. Her lower body seemed to weigh a ton. But finally she was able to prop herself upright on the seat and maintain her balance with a hand held on either side of the *Dolly*.

"Hoist your fanny," Harris directed, and when she did, he shoved the pillow under her rear end. "Gotta take care of those ischial bones, y'know," he teased. He held the oars out to her, and Megan grabbed them automatically. With a mighty groan, Harris flopped into the bottom of the boat and lay there exhausted. "Your turn, matey," he said, and closed his eyes.

The handles of the oars were smooth and warm against Megan's palms. Slowly, she began to row. *I was so sure I'd never ever do this again*, she marveled. Yet here I am, rowing out to a place that I thought would be off-limits to me forever.

Megan felt the muscles across her chest respond to the strain of rowing. The ache felt terrible and wonderful at the same time. Before her, the cottages on Frenchman's Island receded in the distance; when she glanced over her shoulder, she saw the Hideout begin to take shape. White-trunked poplars stood like gleaming arrows against the darkness of the heavier pine woods that grew down the spine of the tiny island. Its slender, curved, white beach shimmered like a gleaming scythe under the noonday sun.

Twenty minutes later, the *Dolly* pressed her bow against the shallow sandbar of the island's shore. Harris, recovered from his brief ordeal, jumped out and pulled the boat far enough up on the sand to anchor it there. "I'll help you out the same way you got in," he announced, and dropped to his knees beside the *Dolly*.

"But this won't be quite as easy," Megan pointed out. "You better drape that blanket over the edge of the boat so I don't accidentally pick up any slivers when you haul me over the side." If that happened it could mean she'd get an infection, which might mean seeing a doctor, which in turn would probably mean taking antibiotics and all that hassle.

As soon as Harris had covered the edge of the boat with the blanket, Megan scooted up to it, leaned over, and looped her arms around his neck, then allowed him to drag her up and out. When he tried to piggyback her up the beach, however, his legs folded under him, and they collapsed together on the sand.

"If we keep doing this, we'll eventually get good at it," he laughed, as they lay gasping side by side. "No offense, M and M, but you're not exactly the easiest girlfriend a guy ever had."

Girlfriend? When had he decided to think of her that way?

"I'm not your girlfriend," Megan corrected firmly. Even when she'd wondered if he was pining for someone at home she'd never imagined that the two of them would be anything except summer friends. "Your friend, maybe, but not your *girlfriend*. Stuff like that isn't part of my life anymore."

Harris rolled over to face her and propped himself up on an elbow. He studied her with pale, kind eyes. "Why not?" he asked bluntly. "Don't get me wrong, M and

M; I didn't bring you out here to put any moves on you—and for sure I don't mean you gotta have a boy-friend—but just think: You believed you'd never come out here again, right? Here you are, though, and you rowed nearly the whole way by yourself! Lighten up, Ms. Murphy. Don't keep closing doors before you've tried to open a few.''

He sat up, took both of her hands, and helped her sit up. ''But I promise to row most of the way home. I need some fuel, though, so what d'you say we eat? I'm starved!''

Without waiting for an answer, Harris spread the blanket across the sand and fetched the canvas bag from the *Dolly*. They ate in contented silence, and just when the sun seemed too warm for comfort, it slipped behind a cloud and the air began to cool. When they were fin-ished, Harris flopped back on the blanket and gave a discreet burp.

'' 'Scuse my bad manners,'' he said, burping a second time, ''but your peanut butter sandwiches would make Sam's Deli blush with shame.''

''Yeah, right,'' Megan snorted, but felt a tickle of satisfaction that he'd said it. Across the water, the two cottages gleamed like a pair of white matchboxes on the shore of Frenchman's Island, their docks invisible at such a distance. From the mainland, the sounds of a calliope at the craft fair drifted across the water. Over-head, gulls called plaintively back and forth. Megan eased herself onto the blanket beside Harris.

''You want to know the last time I looked up at the sky like this?'' she asked. He waited for her to go on.

"On the day of the accident, that's when." Until now, she'd never told anyone what that moment had been like.

"The sky looked just like it does now," she whispered. "Blue, with a few clouds, nothing special, you know? It didn't seem like a day that was going to change my life forever, that nothing anyone could do would ever change it back again."

Harris remained silent. Megan turned to him, eager to tell him more. There was so much to say, things that had gone unsaid for eight months. Harris's lips were slightly parted. His steel-rimmed apothecary's glasses were propped against his breastbone, where the dark shield of sweat on his blue shirt was fading on his narrow chest. His eyes were closed. Red commas marked the spot on either side of his nose where his glasses had rested. Asleep, he didn't look much older than Joey.

"Harris?" Megan called softly, just in case he was faking. He wasn't. He began to make wiffling sounds through his open mouth; no doubt about it, he had zonked.

Megan turned her face back to the sky. So many people—parents, counselors, friends—had told her that life could be good again. She'd never believed them. It'll never happen, she told herself, because I'll never be the person I used to be. But here I am, just like Harris said, she admitted silently, surprised. I'm at the Hideout, a place I didn't think I'd ever see again. I'm here with a summer friend. . . . The sun is warm, and I'm almost happy . . . and very, very sleepy. . . .

* * *

When Megan woke, she turned, her heart hammering, to see that Harris was still dead to the world. The sand beneath her left palm felt cool. Overhead, clouds blocked out the sun. The rising wind had folded an edge of the blanket across her feet. She propped herself upright. The lake was frosted with whitecaps, not the kind that were dangerous. Yet.

She peered toward the middle of the lake. Halfway between Frenchman's Island and the Hideout, something bobbed playfully among the whitecaps, as frisky as a yellow pony grazing in a field of daisies. Megan scanned the beach for the *Dolly*.

The beach was deserted. The *Dolly* was gone.

She touched Harris on the shoulder. It was bony, too, like his knees and spine. "Harris, wake up," she hissed, her mouth as dry as cotton. She poked him harder. "Harris!"

He sat up abruptly, a sheepish expression on his face. He fumbled for his glasses and parked them back on his nose. "Wow, I must've really been pooped," he apologized, yawning and stretching mightily.

What had happened as they slept was so awful that Megan didn't dare look at him. Instead, she pointed toward the middle of the lake. "Look, Harris. Out there." Together, they stared at the bobbing yellow rowboat that grew smaller and smaller as they watched. The *Dolly* moved swiftly toward the opposite shore as surely as if she were drawn there by a magnet.

# 10

Megan glanced down to see Harris's hand creeping toward hers like a crab across the blanket. His fingers trembled when they closed over hers. "It'll be okay, Megan," he promised. "Don't be scared, please." His voice quivered with exactly what he had warned her against.

"It's not your fault, Harris," she told him dully. And it wasn't. It was like the accident. "It just happened," she said. That was true, too. But when would she wise up? Hadn't it been bad enough that the silver web of her spine had been snapped because she had decided to ride home on a cool guy's motorcycle? She hadn't learned a thing, Megan decided, because only a few hours ago, like a fool, she'd urged Harris to "Row away, matey," as if there were nothing to worry about.

Harris nibbled his lower lip. "What I'll do is . . . is . . . I'll swim after the *Dolly* and bring her back!" he announced, brash with courage Megan knew he didn't feel. "She hasn't drifted so far away yet that I won't be able to—"

"Get real, Harris," Megan cut in, her voice ragged with despair. "Just take a look at that sky. Notice that queer green color along the horizon?" He nodded. "That means a storm is blowing up. The *Dolly* would run away from you faster than a greyhound. You'd end up drowning for sure—then I'd be stuck here all alone, with nobody knowing what had happened to either one of us!"

The prospect chilled her with horror. It boggled her mind to imagine being stranded for days here at the Hideout, unable to let anyone know where she was . . . no way to shelter herself from the storm that was coming . . . unable to perform the complicated maneuvers that sometimes were needed to relieve her bowels and bladder. Megan shivered. Starting over? Beginning again? Wretched ideas; she must've been crazy to think they were possible. Megan vowed silently they were mistakes she'd never make a second time.

She noticed that Harris didn't need any further warning to keep him from hurling himself into the foamy surf. Instead, he squatted beside her, his head cradled in his hands. "Well then, what I'll do is . . . is . . . I'll build a fire!" he blurted, fear sharpening his voice until it was as shrill as Joey's when he woke up from a nightmare. "Yeah, right, that's a good idea, because pretty soon it'll be dark, and someone over there in one of the cottages is bound to see it and head over here to rescue us."

"Maybe you're right," Megan agreed, cheered for a moment. Harris slapped at the pockets of his shorts. "Except that I don't have any matches," he groaned.

"But I do," Megan told him. She'd tossed them in with the lunch stuff almost as a second thought on her way out of the kitchen. "I threw some in with our food just before we took off. They're in the bag, probably sifted down to the bottom by now."

Harris snatched up the canvas sack and rummaged around in it. Finally he held up a small box of wooden matches, a relieved smile lighting his pale face. "Hang on to these while I go up into the woods and get some stuff for a fire," he ordered, and when he passed the matches to her, he squeezed her fingers lightly. "Don't melt, M and M," he pleaded. "Trust me, everything's going to be okay."

But as he spoke, an awful realization dawned on Megan. "Harris—there's nobody over there to see our fire," she choked. "Everybody's still at the fair. The only one home right now is Rollie."

Harris stared at her as if she'd slapped his face. He dropped weakly to his knees. "Oh my God," he whispered. Then, brightening, he demanded, "Wait a minute—what time is it?"

Megan checked her watch. "Almost six. So what?"

"So what time is the ferry supposed to make the return trip to Frenchman's Island?"

"About six-thirty," Megan replied, then understood exactly what was on his mind. "But do we have time to build a roaring fire in only half an hour?" she wondered aloud. We? As with so many other things, it could never be we; it would be up to Harris to do it all himself—Harris, whose idea of an outdoor life consisted of going down to Sam's Deli for pastrami on rye with a pickle on the side.

"Hurry up and gather some wood," Megan suggested, "and I'll crunch up our paper cups and the wrappers off our candy bars." She was glad she'd stashed all their trash safely in the empty lunch bag before they'd taken their naps; at least it would give her something to do now while he was gone.

Harris darted up the beach as if he'd been launched out of a cannon, then vanished into the woods that covered the center of the island. While Megan crumpled the wrappers and paper cups, she could hear him thrashing about in the underbrush. She used only half the wrappers and one cup, then sheltered the pieces in her lap to keep them from blowing away and waited for Harris to return.

Moments later, he galloped down the beach, his arms laden with as many twigs and branches as he could carry, his face contorted with distress. "I couldn't find any wood that was real dry," he complained. "Most of this stuff is as green as grass and might not burn worth diddly." He dropped the bundle at his feet and stared at it, disappointed.

"Believe it or not, this might be the best you could've gotten," Megan informed him. "Know what sort of a fire green wood makes? The kind with lots of black smoke, which is exactly what we need to attract the attention of everyone on the ferry."

She handed the stuff on her lap to Harris. "Stack the branches and twigs over these, tepee style," she instructed. "And don't use all the matches trying to get the fire started, just in case we have to try more than once."

The moment Harris touched a match to the candy wrappers, though, they began to burn vigorously. Orange flames soon licked at the damp green twigs. Megan and Harris held their breath, willing the wood to catch fire, then both blinked with despair as it refused to ignite. The flames sputtered anemically, and died.

Harris smacked his forehead. "Jeez, what'll we do now?" he moaned.

Megan plucked the remaining wrappers and the second paper cup out of the lunch bag. "We'll just have to try again," she said. "What'd really help, though, is if we could find some pitch wood to get things started." She squinted thoughtfully toward the woods.

"Pitch wood? What's that?"

"Old wood from a fallen tree, wood that's got streaks of yellow stuff in it. It looks sort of like pulled taffy. You can break it out of the wood and use it to start a fire. It burns hot and fast, almost like charcoal starter."

The words were scarcely out of her mouth before Harris charged back into the woods. Again, Megan could hear him crashing around, and when he returned a few minutes later, he carried a partly decayed pine log that was streaked with amber-colored markings. "Is this what you were talking about?" he wanted to know.

"Way to go!" Megan assured him, then handed him

the freshly crunched candy wrappers and paper cup and watched as he made a new tepee of paper, green twigs and branches, interlacing it with slivers of the golden, streaky wood. When he lighted the paper it burned fitfully, then the pitch splinters began to snap and crackle. Soon, twig by twig, the green wood started to sizzle and burn, too. Before long, the fire delivered exactly what Megan had hoped it would: Long, dark ropes of smoke twisted skyward and soon were strung by the wind across the lake like black rescue cables.

"What a relief!" Harris exclaimed. "Nobody on the ferry'll be able to ignore *that*!" He hesitated uncertainly. "But will they understand what it means?" he worried. "That we're stranded here, y'know? Will they stop right away and pick us up, or—" He cast a furtive glance over his shoulder at the darkening woods, as if he feared that nighttime would bring packs of bears or wolves out of their lairs.

"The ferry won't be able to get too close," Megan answered. "Remember how shallow it was when you pulled the *Dolly* up onto the beach? Well, the ferry draws too much water to be able to get closer to us than maybe a hundred feet offshore. They'll have to drop a dinghy and somebody will have to row over here to get us."

"Drop a dinghy?"

"It's a small boat. There are always several on board; it's a Coast Guard rule, just in case the ferry were to capsize and passengers had to be put off."

Harris shaded his eyes and scanned the horizon, the

wind peeling his hair back from his forehead. He concentrated on the direction from which the ferry ought to approach. "If it gets much darker nobody's going to be able to see our smoke," he agonized out loud.

Megan checked her watch again. "It's not quite seven o'clock," she reported. "Maybe the ferry was delayed on account of the storm."

Harris began to hop anxiously from one foot to the other, like Joey did when he had to go to the bathroom real bad. Suddenly, he stopped dancing. "I think I see it!" he yelled. "Over there, Megan—look!"

Megan craned her neck. "That's it, all right!" she cried, as relieved as he was. "Pile on some more green stuff just to make sure they don't miss us. Get my pillow case off my pillow, too; wave it as hard as you can!"

Harris added more twigs and the ropes of smoke grew blacker and greasier. He stripped the case off her pillow and waved it frantically over his head. Moments later, the ferry passed by and continued to chug toward Frenchman's Island, as indifferent to their plight as a dowager queen to a pair of beggars.

"What'll we do now, Megan?" Harris moaned. "Nobody saw us!" He cast another wary glance at the woods behind them. "D'you think we'll be stuck here all night?" But as he spoke, Megan saw a bright yellow shape drift across the bow of the ferry. The larger boat slowed, coughed asthmatically as the captain cut its engine, then halted altogether.

"They've spotted the *Dolly*," she called to Harris. Oh, if only she could jump to her feet, run into the surf with him, holler and scream and make sure someone saw! She'd have to content herself with sitting on the blanket and holding her arms up in a victory V and be grateful that someone on board—Mom or Joey, probably—had spied the yellow boat and had put two and two together.

It took several minutes for the ferry to turn in the choppy water and then proceed with a grandmotherly harrumph toward the Hideout. Harris threw down the pillow case and grabbed Megan by the shoulders.

"We're gonna be rescued," he whispered against her cheek, "just like I told you we would!" He's even more relieved for himself than for me, she realized as he glanced over her shoulder toward the woods for the third time.

When a dinghy was lowered, Megan saw Mom and Joey climb into it, right behind the cocaptain of the ferry. She cringed inwardly; it was going to be awfully hard to explain to Mom about starting over and beginning again, and most importantly that none of what had happened was Harris's fault.

Ten minutes later, Mom jumped out of the dinghy, landed up to her knees in the sudsy surf, then strode up the beach. Joey followed, the water up to his armpits. Mom ran across the sand, the skirt of her worn, wet, blue chambray sundress slapping against her bare brown legs.

"Meggie, can you imagine what I thought when I saw the *Dolly* floating along—empty, for God's sake!—your chair on the beach and—and the house all dark? What in the name of the sweet Lord are you doing out here?'' She didn't give Harris a glance, a sure sign that she was even more upset with him.

"It was my idea, Mrs. Murphy," Harris spoke up quickly. "I was the one who thought it'd be a neat idea to come over here. I talked Megan into it."

"He didn't talk me into anything," Megan corrected. "I talked myself into it, and everything would've been all right if we'd just made sure to pull the *Dolly* far enough up on the beach so she wouldn't drift away. But the wind came up and she just sort of—''

"Sort of floated off!" Joey finished accusingly. "Jeez, Megan, she could've ended up in . . . in . . . China!''

Mom took a deep breath and was about to go on with her lecture when a second dinghy approached across the gray, rolling water. Andrew rowed, his head tucked down against his breastbone like a bird's in a storm. Julia stood grandly in the bow, the wind flattening her emerald-colored dress against her not-so-lean torso. Even from a distance Megan could hear the musical clank of her bracelets and saw that ribbons of the actress's fiery hair had escaped from beneath the straw hat that she held clamped on her head.

"Hallooo!" Julia cried merrily above the sound of the surf. "I'm *so* disappointed you weren't with us today, Harris. Something quite wonderful happened!" She nearly toppled headfirst out of the dinghy when she swept her hat off her head and waved it gaily back and forth through the spray-filled air.

"I'm going to be in a play!" she called happily. "It's no great thing, you understand, just a little production for a community theater group on the mainland. Someone recognized me at the fair—can you believe it, Harris?—and asked if I'd take a part. It's for charity, so it was easy to say yes." She frowned suddenly, as if a distasteful thought had occurred to her.

"But it's not one of those old-woman parts, mind you, Harris, not in the least. They don't want me to play some terrible old hag!"

Harris leaned past Megan's shoulder as Julia came nearer across the churning water. "Julia," he called back, "Megan and I have been stranded here all afternoon. What if we hadn't been rescued till morning? Or next week? Or at all?" His voice was small and wistful, and Megan realized he was talking about more than being stranded on the island.

Julia, momentarily taken aback by his reproach, fell silent. A moment later she came grandly ashore. "Heavens, Harris, you never were an ordinary little boy, never afraid of the dark or any of those common things!" she exclaimed, recovering herself. "You've always been so old for your age. You just naturally knew how to take care of things—and of me, too," she reminded him briskly, waving away his complaint with a clank of bracelets.

"Why, don't you remember the time we had that fire in our cabin in the Adirondacks? You knew exactly how to call the fire department and gave them such wonderful directions about getting to where we were that they had no trouble finding us at all. Dear boy! I know I never have to worry about *you*!''

Megan remembered the dread she'd heard in Harris's voice when he assumed they might be stranded on the island all night, how he kept glancing furtively toward the woods as if it were full of wild animals that might tear him limb from limb.

*He's not the person Julia thinks he is*, Megan realized. He's been scared of the dark just like any kid. Suddenly, she wondered: What would it be like if nobody ever worried about you? It would probably make you feel lost and lonesome, would make you feel old before you'd had a chance to be a child. It might be a lot worse than having parents who worried about you too much.

Megan studied Harris's profile for a clue as to what was going on in his head. Behind his water-spotted glasses his blue eyes were pale and calm; a tiny smile tugged at the corner of his mouth, but it was a smile of resignation, not happiness. He shrugged lightly, got to his feet, and began to clumsily kick sand over the rescue fire with the side of his foot.

"Listen, Harris," Megan consoled, "I don't think your grandmother meant that exactly the way it came out."

"Yes, she did," he countered in a flat voice. "The famous Julia St. John really has only one major interest in life. Herself." He turned away and walked quickly to the dinghy that had carried Andrew and Julia to shore.

Megan put out her hand to stop him, but she was too late. There was something important she needed to tell him: that she wouldn't be able to see him tomorrow. Or on the day after that. Or for the rest of the summer. Not because what had happened today was his fault; it wasn't. But before he left, she wished she could've explained to him that she'd made a big mistake: She'd thought she could start over, begin again, pick up the pieces. Megan knew now that she'd been wrong. Too bad she wouldn't be able to tell him good-bye.

**11**

"Harris came over this morning to see how you were getting along," Mom announced. Megan watched silently as Mom smoothed lotion on her unfeeling right leg, lifted the leg off the bed, then with smooth, practiced strokes began to massage and flex the inert limb.

Megan turned her face to the wall and didn't answer. She still felt dry and feverish from the bladder infection that had announced itself two days after the rescue from the Hideout. A doctor had to be called over from the mainland, and Megan wanted to die when he walked into the cottage. He looked so young that it was hard to believe he'd graduated from high school, let alone medical school. It was like being examined by a guy from your third-hour biology class. Then to have to discuss with him—a stranger who looked the same age as Dex Cooper—the mechanics of bowels and bladders—arrrggghhh!

"I told Harris you were still asleep," Mom went on, "but that he ought to come back later."

Megan fastened her gaze on the shadows of the leaves outside that were cast on the knotty-pine wall beside her bed. "You shouldn't have said that, Mom," she objected tonelessly.

From the sensation of tightened muscles just below her navel, Megan knew that Mom had finished with the right leg and was beginning to work on the left one. "Why not, Meggie?" she asked, surprised. "Harris seems like such a nice guy—I realize that he wasn't responsible for what happened out there—and I thought that the two of you—"

"The two of us nothing, Mom," Megan corrected, reaching for the insulated mug on her medicine cart. It was filled with ice-cold cranberry juice, and she took a long, slow swallow through a bendable straw.

"The bottom line, Mom, is that I'm never going to be able to do stuff like I used to. Like a regular person, you know? There's no use pretending that I can, not to myself or anyone else. Seeing Harris only reminds me of one thing. Of what I can't be, won't ever be. All we can do, Harris and I, is something safe, like play checkers. Sorry, Mom. I'm *not* a regular person anymore."

Inside, Megan felt exactly as she had when she'd first come home from rehab. *Stay away, world* had been her daily prayer. *Leave me alone, life* had been the second invocation. Everyone out there, if you really want to be nice to me, leave me alone. Don't come to visit; take my name out of your address books; don't bother to call me on the phone. What had happened a few days ago at the Hideout only proved she'd been right.

"Gosh, Meggie, I think you're being too pessimistic,

not to mention too hard on poor Harris," Mom objected. Megan heard her mother's voice crack with regret.

"Face it, Mom. I'm always going to be a patient. I'll always have to worry about when—and where—to empty my bladder. I'll always have to be sure I've lifted my tush off my chair often enough." Megan stared down at her legs.

"Just look what happened because I pretended I'm not different. My legs got a terrible sunburn when I fell asleep for a couple of hours on the beach. As if that weren't bad enough, I got a bladder infection that'll take ten days and a bunch of tetracycline to clear up. All because I wanted to be someone I'll never be again."

Some things she couldn't talk about, though, things that bothered her even more now that she'd had time to think about them. For instance: How had she looked, sprawled there on the sand at the Hideout, her lower body as useless as a corpse's? Or when Harris dumped her into the *Dolly*? Like a beached whale, probably. And she shuddered every time she pondered what it might've been like if they'd actually been stranded out there together even longer. She might've had to ask him for help with bodily functions that ought to be private. It was bad enough when you had to ask your mom for help, like you were a three-year-old who wasn't completely potty trained—but a *guy*? Oh God, life had become so humiliating. . . .

"Ummm," Mom murmured, the sort of *ummm* that meant, "Think it over, Meggie, before you burn all your bridges."

"No way, Mom," Megan insisted. "Tell Harris when

he comes back that I'm still sleeping. Tell him I died. Tell him anything. None of you guys understand that now I've got a body that's like an appliance. It needs constant maintenance. It has to be stretched and oiled and poked and drained, but it can't ever be taken for granted.''

*I don't like my body anymore*, she wished she could explain. *Sometimes I hate it. A lot.*

Mom placed the cap back on the lotion bottle. ''If that's what you've decided, Meggie, I won't argue with you. I'll just tell Harris you're still feeling, well, a little bit under the weather,'' she agreed wistfully. ''Later, when you've had time to think it over, you might decide—''

''No, Mom. No.'' This way, there'd be no other close calls; nothing else embarrassing could happen. Megan deliberately pushed out of her mind the queer look of pain that had crossed Harris's face when Julia ignored his comments about their near disaster at the Hideout. But *Julia is his problem*, she told herself, not mine.

One thing, though, wasn't quite as easy to put out of her mind: the memory of how terrific it'd felt to pull hard against the *Dolly's* oars, how her muscles had strained eagerly across her chest when they'd responded to the challenge of rowing. *Stop it!* Megan scolded herself. *Forget all that. No more Harris. No more sun in her hair. No more wind in her face.*

Mom hadn't been back in the kitchen more than five minutes when Megan heard Harris's light, eager tap on the screen door. She cupped her hands over her ears so she wouldn't be able to hear the fibs that Mom told him. She squinched her eyes tight when she glimpsed him walking slowly back to the Chambliss cottage moments later.

*I'm sorry, Harris*, Megan apologized silently, *but this is the way it's got to be*. No more starting over; the only thing that matters now is endings.


The bladder infection lasted the rest of the week. Megan watched her sunburned legs blister, then peel, leaving them looking more polished and plastic than before. She quit wearing shorts and wore jeans every day, even when it was hot, just so she wouldn't have to look at them.

Finally, she felt good enough to help Mom bake a batch of banana bread. "Put in lots of nuts, the way I like," Joey begged, and when they ate the first warm slices slathered with apricot jam, he added, "I bet Harris sure would like some of this stuff. I don't think his grandma is the kind who bakes anything."

Megan choked, then laughed in spite of herself. "If Julia St. John ever heard you use the dreaded *G* word, Joey, she'd fill your pockets with rocks and drop you off the nearest dock."

Joey frowned. "She better not try," he muttered darkly, buttering a second piece of banana bread. "We're lucky our grandma doesn't think it's weird to be one."

"Grandma Murphy comes from a different planet," Megan agreed. "To her, looking her age isn't a federal crime." She imagined Grandma Murphy in harem pants, with rings on every finger and bracelets up to her elbows, and laughed again.

Joey sidled up to her chair, the corners of his lips bright with apricot jam. "Know something, Megan?" he asked, then suddenly seemed shy.

"What, Joey?" She leaned close, just in case he had a secret to share.

"It's nicer when you're happy," he confided. "Like now. You laughed today, Megan. Twice."

"Oh, jeez, Joey," Megan groaned, stricken. She dabbed at the corners of his mouth with a paper napkin. The little turkey was so right, yet so wrong. "I know I've been a jerk lately," she admitted, refraining from pointing out (as she usually did) that she had plenty of reason to be.

"Slice me another piece of bread, will you?" she asked, and promised herself she'd try to smile more often. She did again, just for practice, when Joey handed her a fresh piece of banana bread. Okay, she'd decided to stay inside the cottage for the rest of the summer, but that didn't mean she had to be a sorehead all the time, right?

And it didn't mean that Mom and Joey had to hang around and keep her company every second, either. It'd be best if they did stuff they liked to do, so Megan made a suggestion. "Why don't you guys go catch a mess of fish for supper?" She'd decided to stay in prison, but they didn't have to do time with her.

Mom and Joey had been gone about an hour when Megan heard a knock on the door. She flinched, and her heart rattled noisily in her chest. Drat! If it was Harris, she'd pretend to be sleeping. Good thing she'd decided to latch the screen as soon as Mom and Joey left. Harris could stand out there and knock until his knuckles turned black; she'd simply refuse to answer. But when Megan peered toward the screen, she didn't see Harris's long, narrow silouette framed there.

Double, triple drat! It was the ample self of Julia St. John that darkened the bright opening. What can *she* want? Megan wondered irritably. She wheeled to the door, unlatched it, then nudged it open with the footrest of her chair.

Julia drew back, startled. "Oh . . . It's you," she gasped. "I was hoping your mother might be—"

"She and Joey decided to go fishing," Megan answered politely. "Did you want something special? Maybe I could help you."

"Something special?" Julia echoed, flustered. "Well, yes. That is, I'd hoped—it's all my own fault, really. You see, I never should've let both Andrew and Harris go off this morning and leave me with no help. I realize it's a bit to ask, but I thought if your mother could—"

"Did Andrew and Harris go fishing, too?" Megan inquired, unable to imagine what else they might be doing.

"No, no; they both had errands to do on the mainland. I had expected them back by lunchtime, but apparently they couldn't get on the noon ferry and now won't be back until late." Smoke from Julia's cigarette wafted through the doorway, and Megan coughed discreetly.

"Oh, sorry," Julia apologized, dropping the half-smoked cigarette on the porch and squashing it under the heel of her gold sandal. "The thing is, you see, both Harris and Andrew know how to read for me, but since they're both gone, I thought your mother might be able to help me out," Julia murmured, pacing restlessly back and forth across the narrow landing.

"They read to you?" Megan repeated, puzzled.

"Lines, lines!" Julia exclaimed impatiently. "They help me memorize my lines by prompting me when I need it, and by reading the other characters' parts for me."

"Oh, you mean you need a reader," Megan said.

Julia gave her a sharp glance. "What do *you* know about being a reader?" she demanded.

Megan remembered her vow to smile more often and managed a feeble one for Julia's benefit. She pressed the screen door open further. "I was a reader last year for our class play," she answered. That was before the accident, of course. "It was sort of fun."

"Ummm," Julia murmured distractedly, her gaze flicking to the wheelchair and quickly away again.

"If you'd like, maybe I could help you," Megan offered.

"Well . . ." Once again, the actress considered the wheelchair as if it were a living, unpredictable beast. Then she studied the lake, obviously hoping Harris and Andrew would suddenly appear on its surface and rescue her from her dilemma.

"Perhaps you haven't fully recovered from your ordeal on that little island—what did Harris call it—the

110

Hideout?'' Julia murmured, offering Megan an excuse to rethink her offer. ''So I don't want to ask you to do anything that would be—''

''Actually, I'm feeling much better now,'' Megan assured her, remembering that was not the message Mom had delivered to poor Harris. Gingerly, Julia stepped through the doorway. She held a script out to Megan, managing to not quite fasten her glance on the wheelchair as she did so.

''If you're quite sure it will be no bother . . .'' she said uncertainly.

''No, really, I'd like to be your reader,'' Megan said quickly. ''Which scene did you want to work on?''

''Ummm . . . the third in act one,'' Julia murmured, still not at ease. She darted past the chair as if it might leap at her with open jaws. ''It's the one where Gregory and I argue about Abby. She's my competition for Gregory's attention, you see. Gregory and Laura have known each other for years and Laura—that's me—is determined to marry him. He was willing, more or less, until Abby came along, a snip of a girl he thinks he's fallen in love with. Not that Laura is *old*, mind you,'' Julia pointed out hastily. ''She and Gregory are about the same age, sort of . . . ummm . . . middle-aged. So let's start at the top of the page, just after Abby has run out of the room, dissolved in tears again.''

Megan quickly found the place and began to read Gregory's lines, lowering her voice to imitate a man. ''Good heavens, Laura, what did you say to poor Abby this time?''

Julia whirled in the center of the living room and confronted an imaginary Gregory. "Abby, Abby, always Abby! Is she the only one you can think about anymore, Gregory? What about me?" Julia demanded huskily. "I loved you long before you went off to war and even more now that you've come back, darling," she added, and leaned yearningly toward her invisible lover. "Remember how it was for us when we first met, Gregory? Remember?"

Megan stared at the woman poised in the middle of the room. She wasn't the same Julia who'd come through the kitchen door fifteen minutes ago. She was Laura now, and the ravaged lines in her face were softened with longing, her green eyes glowed with an inner fire, and her hair seemed less the color of iodine than of polished bronze. She was, well, almost beautiful.

"Laura, Laura," Megan read, "you've got to accept the fact that it's over between us. I'm beginning a new chapter in my life, and you must be brave enough to do the same. We can't go back, Laura, dear. We can't pretend—"

"We don't have to pretend, Gregory!" Laura/Julia exclaimed in a voice as rich and thick as warm fudge. "What I feel for you can be enough for both of us. A new chapter? Yes, my darling, and we can write it together. Tomorrow could be the beginning of forever, my sweet!" The actress's words were now feverish with desire, which roused Rollie from his nap on the sofa.

"Ah, my lovely, determined Laura, don't you know there's no such thing as forever?" Megan read softly, knowing exactly what Gregory meant.

112

Laura/Julia held her arms out to the empty air, arms that suddenly looked willowy and almost young. "Yes, there is, Gregory," she insisted. "Forever is a place in my heart, a place that belongs only to you!" She stepped forward, nearer the couch, and tenderly folded an imaginary Gregory in a loving embrace. Rollie studied her anxiously, then scooted to the far end of the sofa, his ears flattened to his head. When Julia collapsed happily on the other end of it, Rollie hid his face in his paws.

"Thank you, dear," she breathed happily. "The scene is coming along very well and . . . ummm . . . you were so sweet to help me out." She narrowed her green eyes, and Megan realized that perhaps the actress was seeing her for the first time. "Being a good reader is rather an art, you know, and I must say you did very well," she murmured.

Megan felt her cheeks flush with pleasure. It had been a long while since anyone had any reason to tell her she'd done something well. "I'll help you again, if you'd like," she offered.

But Julia leaped off the sofa before the offer was cool on the air and began to pace restlessly up and down the room. "I didn't know how much I missed it," she confessed, but Megan had the impression that she was speaking more to herself than to any listener.

"Missed acting, I mean," Julia mused. "And what I miss most about it is the *act* in *acting*. It's a verb, you know, just like *work* is a verb. It's also a way for me to be something I'm not, to get outside myself, to be better—or worse—than I really am. The other things—the parties, the reviews, the TV interviews—all that came after the important part, which was to act. To act—it's something I always assumed I'd be able to do forever and ever!''

Julia whirled about, her eyes wide with surprise, as if she'd never intended to reveal so much about herself. Her green glance whisked nervously across the wheelchair, its footrests, its Velcro straps. ''But of course I'm speaking about something you don't understand,'' she said coolly.

''Of course,'' Megan agreed. It would take too long to explain that she understood only too well.

You miss the *act* in acting, she could have told Julia, and I miss the *me* in me. I miss being able to be a reader for the class play again. Miss being able to be a basketball wizard. Miss the me who was my parents' strong, long-legged daughter who could swim and fish and water-ski, who would someday go away to college, coach a girl's basketball team someplace, get married eventually, have kids. What I miss is a chance to be all the things that I know I'll never have a chance to be.

''Gregory told Laura there's no such thing as forever,'' Megan reminded Julia. ''Maybe he was right.''

''Don't say that!'' Julia cried, and Megan was startled by the heartache in the actress's voice. ''That was only a silly line in a silly play; it's not for real! Of course some things are forever!'' She scooped her script off Megan's lap and fled through the door, scaring Rollie so badly that he dived off the sofa and crawled behind it.

*Why did I have to say that?* Megan asked herself. I

guess I wasn't really talking to Julia; I was talking to myself. But Gregory had told the truth: There was no such thing as forever, and the moment she'd read his words to Julia, Megan knew it. My old life would've changed even without the accident, she realized suddenly. So many things would've happened: Bev might've moved away. . . . Dad might've lost his job. . . . I might not have made the team again . . . and that collection of happenings would've meant I'd have ended up being different anyway, even without Dex Cooper's help.

Next door, Megan heard Julia let the door of the Chambliss cottage slam loudly behind her. She watched the sun slide toward the horizon and wished Mom and Joey would hurry home.

A scratching sound on the deck outside tempted Rollie out from behind the sofa. Had Mom and Joey gotten home? Megan wondered, then the welcoming smile froze on her face. This time, it *was* Harris who waited, and she didn't have to look up at him, either.

He was sitting on the landing. In a wheelchair.

**12**

"Is this your idiotic idea of a joke?" Megan demanded, pointing at Harris's chair. "Some sense of humor you've got, Harris. Take my advice, Mr. Smart Aleck St. John—don't go for a career in comedy!"

It was an insult: Just when she'd made up her mind to be exactly what she was—disabled—Harris had decided to pretend to be something he wasn't. Talk about a no-win summer. Megan glared at him and was pleased to see that he shriveled under her stare. Fine; let him shrink until he was the size of a peanut.

Harris's cheeks flushed brightly under his tan, and he began to fidget in his chair. "Listen, I'm not trying to be funny," he protested. "This isn't a joke. Look—" He bent and eagerly pulled up the left leg of his jeans. His normally skinny, brown ankle was plump with a pink elastic bandage.

"It's only a slight sprain," he apologized, as if he were sorry not to have a truly gruesome injury to display.

"It happened this morning when Andrew and I went over to the mainland. I jumped off the ferry onto the dock, and I guess I landed crooked. Andrew hauled me over to that same drop-in clinic where we took Julia the day she whacked her head."

Megan felt her lip curl. "I never heard of a person being put in a wheelchair for a 'slightly' sprained ankle," she scoffed. "My best friend, Bev, sprained hers real bad, and all they gave her was a pair of crutches." She didn't explain that now Bev was an ex-friend. The fact that she and Bev hadn't spoken to each other for months was none of Harris's business.

Harris nodded sheepishly. "Yeah, the doctor over there told me crutches were all I'd need, too," he admitted. "But when Andrew and I went over to the medical supply center to rent a pair, I saw this thing and decided to find out . . ." He hesitated, and Megan was amazed to see his cheeks flush even redder than before.

"To find out what?" Megan demanded suspiciously.

"Well, what it's like for you," he confessed in an embarrassed voice. Megan stared at him with fresh disgust. The light reflected off his glasses prevented her from seeing the expression in his eyes. Was he smirking? Did he think somehow that his idea was clever, that it showed what a sensitive guy he was? "I figured if I spent a little while in this thing, maybe I'd, you know, find out what you have to put up with," he finished awkwardly.

"So?" Megan snapped. "Do you think you do?"

"A little bit, I guess."

117

"And that's all you'll ever know, Harris—just a little bit. Know why?" Megan challenged. Harris shook his head glumly. "Because for you it's only for a few days, until you get tired of doing it. For me, it's the rest of my life. For you, it's a goofy summer pastime; for me, it's forever." She dismissed him with an angry chop of her hand. "Now if you don't mind, Harris, I've got better things to do than sit here explaining the obvious."

When Harris squirmed in his chair the glare on his glasses was suddenly erased. Looking into his blue eyes, Megan saw that he was as sincere about his dumb wheelchair as he was about everything else. The dork *really* did want to know. What to do with a guy like him? It was her turn to hesitate. One thing you had to admit about Harris, though: He wasn't running away, like Dex Cooper had.

Something else dawned on Megan. It made a big difference to talk to a person who wasn't standing over her, talking down at her. With Harris in a wheelchair just as she was, she could look him straight in the eye. Otherwise, it seemed that she was always craning her neck up at people or had to fasten her glance on somebody's belt buckle or belly button. It wasn't funny, but the thought of Harris's belly button made her laugh.

"I thought you said I wasn't much of a comedian," Harris reminded her. "Forget about making a career out of it, you told me."

"And I meant it," Megan giggled helplessly, "but I guess my sense of humor is getting as weird as yours."

"Well, at least you're not mad at me anymore,"

Harris said, and without waiting to be invited, nudged his chair past hers, through the doorway, into the kitchen. Once he was inside, Megan amazed herself by offering, "Hey, you want some banana bread? Mom and I made some for Joey this morning."

Sitting side by side in the twilit kitchen, munching on slices of banana bread that had been warmed in the microwave and drizzled with butter, Megan listened to herself tell Harris about Bev, about Dex, about the basketball game she'd played the week before the accident when she'd personally scored twenty-seven points for the Hudson Hornets.

Then, since it was still strange to see him in a wheelchair, Megan gave in to the temptation to tease him. "Why should I be surprised to see you in that thing?" she asked slyly. "You're Julia St. John's grandson, after all; why wouldn't you have a natural flair for the dramatic?"

At the mention of Julia's name, Harris clapped a hand to his forehead. "Speaking of whom, I better get outa here!" he mumbled. "She wanted some help with her lines today, but Andrew and I were gone longer than we planned. You know Julia; she wants what she wants when she wants it. She's probably had a stroke by now."

"Not to worry," Megan said airily.

"Are you kidding? Believe me, this is worry time! Julia hasn't had a part in anything for so long that she'll need to rehearse her brains out. This play may be a charity gig, nothing to get in a tizzy about, but neither Andrew nor I want her to get up in front of everybody and make a fool out of herself—which, considering that memorizing lines has always been hard for her, is a distinct possibility.''

''She won't make a fool out of herself,'' Megan promised. ''She's going to be just great, just like my mom says she's always been. Anyway, she already rehearsed today.''

Harris frowned. ''Who with? Your mom?''

''No. With me.''

''*You?*''

''I was the only one around,'' Megan explained. ''It was me or nobody. She did her best to ignore the fact that I'm in this thing.'' She patted the arm of her chair. ''Which, come to think of it, brings up an interesting point. If my chair makes her nervous, what's yours going to do to her?''

Harris groaned. ''Believe me, I thought about it,'' he admitted. ''Andrew did, too.'' He rubbed the arms of his chair thoughtfully, a gesture that haunted Megan with its familiarity. Then she realized why: It was what she so often did herself—rub, rub, rub, as if a genie could be called out, a genie who might grant her the wish to be Megan the Magnificent again.

Harris, however, was thinking of Julia, not genies. ''How'd she act today?'' he wanted to know. ''She's been getting more and more uptight over this whole thing; you'd think it was the role of a lifetime. She keeps telling Andrew and me that she's only doing this as a favor to the lady who recognized her at the fair, but once you've been a star . . .''

"I think Julia will always be a star," Megan said quietly, remembering how eager and alive the actress had been as she transformed herself into Laura. "She told me she missed the act in acting," Megan went on, "and I think I know exactly what she meant." Maybe for Julia, it was like what the counselors at rehab had said, that there'd be good days and bad days, days when it was easy to forget what had happened, days when it was impossible not to remember that the ache of who you used to be would be as sharp as it was at the beginning.

Harris leaned forward in his chair. "Maybe it'll work for her," he confided. "When we get home maybe she'll start reading parts that fit her instead of trying to be Juliet forever. And maybe"—he gave Megan a sad, throwaway smile that made him seem even younger than Joey—"she might realize that Andrew and I are alive, too, and quit acting like such a crazy lady."

Megan sat up straighter. "She's not a crazy lady," she objected warmly, surprised to hear herself sticking up for Julia.

"Oh, I don't mean crazy crazy," Harris explained. "But at home she'd started doing some pretty goofy stuff. Like she wanted people to pay attention to her, but she'd never leave the apartment. Or if we did go out, she'd never go to the places we always used to go. Why else do you think we ended up on Frenchman's Island this summer? No matter what she said, it wasn't Andrew's idea or mine, either; she wanted to go to a place where nobody knew her. She's started calling herself The Once Great and Famous and keeps the draperies in the apartment pulled all day. Smokes too much. Watches too much TV. Starts drinking sherry earlier and earlier every afternoon.''

Harris peered at her through the gloom of the evening kitchen, and Megan realized he was trying to tell her something else. ''Julia put herself in jail and threw away the key,'' he said, and sighed. ''Trouble is, she locked me and Andrew up with her.''

Megan wished he hadn't told her so much. Such revelations made her squirm. Julia refused to go anywhere . . . craved attention that once had been her due . . . kept her family locked up as if the three of them were cell mates.

And I've done the same thing, Megan realized. Maybe that's why I'm sticking up for her—because we're exactly alike.

Harris cleared his throat. Megan suddenly wished Mom and Joey would burst through the door, flick on all the lights, and chase the evening shadows away, shrinking life back to familiar proportions.

''Actually, I didn't come by to talk about Julia,'' Harris apologized, as if he could read her thoughts. ''I really stopped to give you this.'' He reached into his pocket. ''I saw it at the medical-supply place where I rented the chair and thought maybe you'd be interested,'' he added casually. Too casually, Megan decided a moment later. He dropped the square of orange paper into her lap.

Megan smoothed it across her knees and began to read. The letters on the flyer were bold and black. COME

TO THE HANDIFAIR! GO FOR THE GOLD, ALL YOU WHEELCHAIR RACERS! THIS SANCTIONED EVENT WILL EARN POINTS TOWARD YOUR ALL-STATE SCORES. SEE Y'ALL ON THE FIRST SUNDAY IN AUGUST!

She stared first at the flyer, then at Harris. An old, cold, bitter feeling pinched her heart, made it hard and unforgiving. The skin across her cheeks felt suddenly taut and dry. The taste in her mouth was metallic, like the taste of the pennies she'd sucked when she was a kid.

*He tricked me*, she realized. He pretended to rent that chair so he could find out what it was like to be disabled, but all the while he was plotting to interest me in something else. He wants me to try something I'm not ready for yet.

"You rented that wheelchair . . . so you'd have an excuse . . . to drop this bomb on me," Megan accused haltingly. She waved the orange paper slowly under Harris's nose. "Well, Harris, I'm not your summer hobby. If you want one, stick to running Julia's life. I don't need any help running mine."

Push-pull; try-fail; two moves forward, one move back; that's what the whole summer had turned into. But I can't hack it anymore, Megan decided. Can't. Won't. Don't want to.

She jockeyed her chair around so hard that she locked her footrests with Harris's. As she struggled to pry herself loose she felt tears scald her cheeks. Great; on top of all the other humiliations, now she was going to bawl. Her eyes would swell up, her beak would get as red as

Rudolph's, her nose would run like Joey's did when he stubbed his toe.

"I'm not going . . . to haul myself . . . around some stupid track . . . with a bunch of people . . . who are trying to convince themselves . . . they're doing something that matters," she choked. "The only sports that count are the real kind, played by people with legs. Get out of my way, Harris. Get out of my life. Go play Robinson Crusoe with someone else!"

Harris backed himself onto the landing and sat there, hunched and forlorn. Gregory had been wrong, Megan realized suddenly; it was Laura who'd been right after all: Some things *did* last forever.

**13**

"Megan!" Joey cried as he rushed in from the beach. In five brief weeks he'd turned from winter white to summer brown. His vanilla-colored hair had become paler than ever, and his freckles, which had been solitary chocolate chips at the beginning of summer, were melted into a smooth, milk-chocolate frosting across the back of his thin neck.

"Megan!" he yelled again. "Did Harris tell you?"

Megan stiffened. Harris, Harris; she wished Julia would decide she couldn't stand life on Frenchman's Island and would leave in a snit, taking dear old Harris with her. The guy had gotten to be like a bad smell that couldn't be washed away.

"Did Harris tell me what, Joey?" Megan asked warily, certain that she didn't want to hear one more word about Mr. St. John's bright ideas. On the other hand, staying mad day after day had turned out to be harder work than she'd imagined. It didn't help, either, that now Joey might be trying to sabotage her determination to stamp CANCEL across the rest of the summer.

"About those wheelchair races!" Joey exclaimed. "Harris got you an application and everything."

Ah; now he even had an application.

Tell me some news that's new, Megan considered retorting, but there was no reason to dump on Joey.

"Harris says he can't compete, that him being in a wheelchair doesn't count, but you could." Joey danced in front of her, his eyes blazing with anticipation. "We could go watch you, Megan, just like we did when you played basketball and stuff."

"Get out of my face, Joey," Megan warned, her own eyes blazing. She raised a palm to fend off his enthusiasm. Harris had put that bug in Joey's ears on purpose, she realized. He hoped to make an ally out of her brother, to make Joey a booster of his own fabulous ideas.

"But Harris said—"

"If you'll notice, Joey, Harris is always saying something," Megan pointed out. "Now you can tell *him* something. Tell him the counselors in the rehab unit said it was up to me how fast—or slow—I adjusted to this." She tapped her kneecaps significantly. "Nobody ever said anything about a rehabilitation program cooked up by anyone named Harris St. John, okay? They didn't tell me anything about wheelchair races, either. If Harris is disappointed, too bad. That's his problem, not mine."

"But . . . but . . . Harris said you could get some points or something if you'd just—"

"Points, schmoints. Tell Harris to stop already—and you stop, too, Joey."

Joey rubbed one bare, crusty, foot on top of the other. "Anyway, that isn't even why I came in," he mumbled sullenly, his chin resting on his collarbone.

"So why did you then?"

"Julia sent me."

"Julia?" Megan groaned under her breath. Had Harris enlisted Julia to his cause, too?

"She wants you to help her again," Joey went on, balancing himself on one leg like a crane. "She says you're better than Harris or Andrew."

"Better? At what?"

"You know," he said crankily, "reading stuff to her. She says you've got flair. Whatever that is. She says she's got a whatchamacallit—a dress rehearsal—and that's why she's gotta practice extra hard today."

"So what's Harris-baby doing as we speak?" Megan demanded suspiciously. "Why can't he help her?"

"Julia said he's resting. His ankle hurts, she said. He's got to take aspirin for it."

Okay, reading I can handle, Megan thought, relieved. And if Harris was sick in his room, so much the better. "Tell her I'll be over in a jiff," she told Joey. But of course nothing could be done in a jiff anymore, and it was nearly twenty minutes before she'd finished in the bathroom and could wheel herself out the back door.

Rolling along the quiet, dappled path behind the cottages, however, Megan found herself thinking more about racing than reading.

Racing. Would it be anything like rowing? Would pulling hard on the handrims, forcing her chair to move faster and faster, make her feel as she had when she'd rowed Harris out to the Hideout two weeks ago? Would it make her feel as she had when she went into the air to lay up a shot in a close game against the Rockettes?

Megan crouched over her knees, gripped both handrims and gave each one a single strong, hard stroke. Her chair leaped forward like a deer that had been startled out of the woods. She was glad no one was around to see the smile that plastered itself all over her face. Exhilaration flooded her chest, her arms, her fingertips. Okay, so it wasn't exactly like dunking a basket in the final ten seconds of a game; nothing ever would be, right? But jeez—it felt great!

Once again, Megan leaned experimentally across her knees; once again, her chair leaped gladly forward, and the breeze created by her flight down the path lifted her pale, brief bangs off her forehead. If Harris wanted to play a summer game, well, why not play with him? Why not give him the shock of his life by taking up his challenge?

Megan slowed as she approached the Chambliss cottage. There'd been magazines at the counselor's office, she remembered, with pictures on their covers of people in wheelchairs, chairs that looked much different than her own. The chairs in those photos had been stripped of all but their most essential parts, to make them lighter weight and more aerodynamic.

"The New Mag Magic," a legend under one such

picture had read, and in a sidebar, "Inside: Read about the Latest in Wheelchair Racing Technology!" The chair to be discussed was made out of an alloy of magnesium, she recalled. At the time, there'd been no reason to be interested in whether it was made out of magnesium or marshmallows. Yet nagging uncertainty wouldn't let Megan alone: How could people in wheelchairs do *real* sports? Telling yourself they could—wasn't that just another mind game, another way of trying to make you forget you'd never do the best kind again?

Megan hoped Joey had been right that Harris was resting; even though she was beginning to tinker with the idea of racing, she didn't want to have to face him yet. Come to think of it, she didn't need his help to enter the race. Mom could pick up an application; Harris wouldn't have to be involved at all. But no sooner had she rounded the sharp corner leading up to the back entry of the neighboring cottage than she saw him parked right there in his dumb wheelchair, a book on his knees. He turned, surprised, then grinned, inspiring her to scowl darkly at him.

"Give it up, Harris," she said, pointing at his chair. "Anybody'd think you'd sprained both ankles instead of only one."

Harris shrugged. "I rented it for two weeks so I'm going to get my money's worth," he answered, ignoring her sarcasm. That was something else that bugged her about him: Harris never seemed to get ticked off, like a normal person. He was always pleasant, even-tempered, saintly. Yuk!

"How's Julia handling it? Your chair, I mean?" Megan demanded, hoping to make him squirm.

Harris shrugged. "She's been too busy lately to pay much attention to it," he answered evenly.

"Well, you better tell her I'm here so we can get started practicing," Megan sniffed. "I can't very easily get up onto this stoop, so I guess we'll have to read down here." But as she glanced toward the Chambliss back door, Megan saw that two wide boards had been laid up against the stoop and were designed to act as a makeshift ramp.

"Andrew and I fixed that up," Harris explained, "but the pitch is kinda steep so you better let me help you." He hopped out of his chair, limped around behind her, and gave her a brisk shove.

Megan turned to him, a triumphant smirk on her face. "There—you just proved my point! *You* can quit being disabled any time you want, Harris; *I* can't."

Harris leaned toward her, and Megan was shocked to see a black, disgusted look contort his usually bland face. "But do you want to know what you *can* do, M and M?" he challenged in a cool-as-a-Popsicle voice. "You could quit feeling so doggone sorry for yourself. With you, it's getting to be a real art; anybody'd think you were the only person in the whole world who'd ever had anything bad happen to her."

Megan stared, stunned into wordlessness. Harris knelt clumsily in front of her chair, his pale eyes hard. "Know how old I was when my folks were killed? Only six; I'd been in the first grade for three whole weeks. My mom and dad won't ever know what kind of a person I turned out to be, and I'll never have a chance to know them, either.

"How about Julia? For sure she never planned to be a mother twice, but she got stuck in the middle of her life with a little kid who could be a pain in the neck. She's tormented herself for years with each new wrinkle, and has made Andrew and me into a pair of prisoners with no hope of parole. Speaking of Andrew—listen, his first wife died of cancer, an inch at a time, and it broke his heart."

Harris paused, but his eyes remained stony. "Go ahead and hang your accident around your neck like it's a medal, Megan Murphy. Just don't expect the rest of the world to go on forever congratulating you on your fine achievement."

With each of his words, Megan felt heat rise from her chest and color her face a deeper shade of scarlet. What colossal nerve! Who was he to give lectures, he who had two perfectly good legs, knobby-kneed and skinny for sure, but at least they worked? He made it sound as if she were a crybaby for no good reason. Even the people at the rehab unit, who could be tough as nails, had never gone this far.

"You've got no right—" she began, but couldn't continue her defense because Julia burst onto the deck in a flurry of brilliant fabric and jangle of bracelets. She wore beach pajamas again, this time in shades of pink and purple, but otherwise looked to be quite a different woman.

131

Her glittering green eyes were no longer smudge pots of mascara. She wore only a light touch of eyeshadow, and her rouge was discreetly applied so that her cheeks no longer resembled the taillights of a late-model car on a dark night.

"Darling!" she cried merrily, causing Megan to wonder when she'd been promoted from being a dear to being a darling. "Andrew and Harris would've been glad to help me, the sweeties, but I told them you're such a divine reader that I'd rather have you. And I've quite forgiven you for reminding me that Gregory might've been right about forever!" She swept across the deck, as graceful as someone much younger, and dropped the manuscript into Megan's lap. "Do come in; let's get started right away." She dismissed Harris with an airy wave. "We'll make the fellows stay outdoors until we're finished," she said, and held the door open for Megan to pass through.

Inside, Megan was surprised to see that the draperies across the Chambliss living room had been pulled aside and light flooded the room. Beyond the windows stretched a swath of golden beach, and farther away across the blue water was the Hideout. Megan was grateful to be able to tear her eyes from it when Julia urged, "Let's start at the top of page eighty-one." Better not to look at the Hideout, or be reminded of Harris's recent lecture.

"This is one of my big scenes," Julia explained. "In it, Abby accuses me of telling lies to get my way with Gregory, but I'm denying there's any truth in what she says."

Megan took a breath and began to read Abby's lines. "Laura, you've always had a gift for thinking only of yourself. You're not truly thinking of Gregory at all, only of what *you* want."

"Nonsense," Laura objected, and Julia drew herself into a regal pose as she spoke. "It's fate that drew us together in the beginning, my dear, and it's fate that will keep Gregory and me together in the end." She lowered her voice to a silky purr. "You may be young and pretty, Abby, but youth and beauty aren't everything. You see, I *understand* Gregory, something you might never be able to do."

"Is that why you lied to him? Told him I didn't love him? It's Gregory who must decide for himself what he wants," Megan read. "He's not a pawn, Laura. He's a person who has the right to understand his own heart, not be told by someone else what is good or bad for him."

"Foolish, foolish child!" Laura chided, pacing the length of the Chambliss living room. Julia had committed her lines firmly to memory, Megan realized, which gave her greater freedom to inject into her role all the craft and passion she'd acquired during forty years of acting. The long scene ended when Abby, defeated once again and in tears, fled from the stage. "Such a silly fool!" Laura exclaimed in a husky, victorious whisper as soon as Abby was gone. "Gregory has always belonged to me—and he always will!"

Standing in the middle of the living room, Julia paused to hug herself with childish delight. "Oh, it's coming along famously, darling! I thought I'd have trouble getting my lines branded into my brain but I haven't, not a bit.'' She pressed her palms to her newly pale cheeks.

"I have to confess that I was rather afraid," she admitted in a husky whisper. "Can you imagine—Julia St. John, who's got awards galore on her mantel—being afraid of a charity performance for a community theater group? But I haven't done anything professionally for so long, you see, that I'd gotten rusty. . . .''

Julia hesitated and fixed Megan with an intense green gaze. "In the play, Laura talks about fate; have you ever wondered about it yourself?'' She leaned close. "What if I had refused your mother's invitation to go to the craft fair? I almost did, you know. It would've meant I'd never have met that woman who invited me to participate in the production of *Call Back Yesterday*. Fate—it's such a quirky thing, don't you think?''

The question hung on the air, demanding an answer. "I guess so,'' Megan said uneasily. Then Julia banished the troubling subject as quickly as she'd brought it up. "Now I hope you're planning to come to opening night, Megan, dear. You've given me such important help, and I want you to share it with me.''

"Ummm, maybe,'' Megan replied uncertainly. Opening night? It would mean going out in public . . . wheeling herself into an auditorium. . . . People would stare. . . . The experience might turn out to be as horrible as the one and only time she'd gone back to Hudson. Megan lowered her glance and pretended to inspect her watch. "Gee, I better get home now,'' she mumbled, eager to escape the new Julia and her infectious optimism.

Julia swept some tickets off the coffee table and dropped them into Megan's lap. "These freebies were given to me, and I want you and your parents—Joey too, of course—to come."

"But there are five tickets here," Megan pointed out.

"One of them is for Harris. You see, Andrew and I will have to leave early, and if you'd all be good enough to let Harris come with you, I'd be most appreciative."

Harris again; always Harris around some corner somewhere. Megan stuffed the tickets in her pocket, then scooted out the door and rolled herself as noiselessly as possible down the two-board ramp at the end of the Chambliss deck, anxious not to attract the attention of Harris and Andrew, who sat facing the lake.

Have you ever wondered about fate? Julia had asked.

As if there were any way I could not wonder, Megan thought ruefully. She didn't race home, but instead rolled slowly along the back pathway. The afternoon had been one of those in which too much had been said and heard, like the early days at rehab when she'd gotten too much advice, too much encouragement, too much of everything. Megan struggled to sort out the words and thoughts in her head, but the ones that refused to be cataloged were Harris's.

*Hang your accident around your neck like it was a medal*, he'd scoffed.

Megan stopped in the middle of the path. From above, the two squirrels scolded her; the late-afternoon sun dappled the path; Mom was making spaghetti and the smell of its fragrant, garlicky sauce floated through the kitchen window.

Fate. Had it knocked again, not in the form of an accident, but in the shape of a chance to enter a wheelchair race?

Megan took a deep breath, bent forward, and gave her chair a hard stroke. Once again, the chair leaped forward like a deer. Once again, Megan couldn't subdue the thrill that blossomed like a sunflower in her chest, and smiled in spite of herself.

**14**

It could be counted as yet another one of those queer, unnatural moments the counselors had warned her about, Megan decided as she rolled herself up the loading ramp onto the ferry.

Just when you thought the period of adjustment was over, that you'd gotten used to the new way you had to do things, they cautioned, something would bring back memories of how you used to do it. When that happened, your grief would be as fresh and sharp as ever.

And it was. Other years, for instance, she'd done exactly as Joey was doing now—charged the length of the loading ramp full tilt, then galloped to the rail to hang over. She'd stood with him there, watched the wake as it churled and foamed when the ferry pulled away from the dock, and held up bread crusts to the gulls that hovered close, greedy for such handouts.

Now, as she wheeled slowly up the ramp, pushing hard against the incline, a light sweat moistened

Megan's neck and chest. It didn't really help that Harris hobbled up beside her on his new crutches. She regretted now that she'd chewed him out about the wheelchair and wished he hadn't taken her at her word. If he hadn't, they'd have wheeled side by side into the auditorium and would have shared the stares of the other playgoers. Being the only one in a wheelchair meant she'd be the focus of everyone's attention, which had been the problem at Hudson too—no one else in the whole place had been handicapped, and she'd felt like a freak.

They all got into the car when it was unloaded on the opposite side of the lake, and Dad drove through the twilit countryside to the community theater on the outskirts of Aurora. "Hey, I thought we were going to a play!" Joey exclaimed when Dad parked the car in front of a stone barn on the edge of a fragrant field of alfalfa. "This looks like somebody's farm to me!"

"We *are* going to a play, Joey," Mom assured him with a shush. "The acting group has converted this old barn into a theater. Look; see what it says up there?" She pointed to a colorful sign that had been mounted just below what once were a pair of hayloft doors.

" 'The Playhouse,' " Joey read aloud, scowling. "Sounds like a place where a bunch of dorky girls dress up in old clothes and play dolls!"

"Well, it isn't," Megan informed him. "This is where Julia might make a comeback."

"Don't I hope," Harris murmured in a subdued voice. "She was so sure of herself when she and Andrew left this afternoon that it scared me. I mean, what if she was just a little *too* confident?"

138

Megan gave him a sharp glance. What had he seen that made him so full of gloom and doom? She remembered her first introduction to Julia when the actress had reeled and swayed in the doorway of the Chambliss cottage. Was it possible Julia had been messing around with mouthwash again?

Rows of cars had been parked in the twilit fields of clover that surrounded The Playhouse, and theatergoers drifted toward the old barn, their pale summer clothes mothlike in the dusk. Their laughter was liquid and expectant, and hearing it Megan felt her heart beat a little faster. She was glad it was evening; in such soft light maybe her wheelchair would be less noticeable.

Inside, Mom and Dad and Joey filed into their seats, clutching their programs, and Harris sat in the aisle seat. When most of the audience had been seated, Megan parked her chair in the aisle next to Harris. The houselights went down, and the audience settled itself. There seemed to be an unusual flurry of activity behind the curtains, then music began to waft over the heads of the playgoers to mask the commotion backstage.

Megan felt her hands go clammy. Had something happened to Julia even before the play got under way? She was relieved when the curtains parted and she saw Gregory and Abby greeting each other for the first time since his return from the war. Looking at Abby, Megan felt a sudden stab of pain.

She was beautiful! Her blue dress was the stuff dreams were made of, her hair was a mass of pale gold curls, her skin as perfect as the surface of a porcelain figurine. She was everything Julia probably once had been: tall,

139

slim, lovely, and—most of all—young. Hastily, Megan consulted her program. In real life, Abby was Jean Monroe, a part-time librarian from Aurora and mother of two preschool children. But onstage she was everything Abby, the lovely young girl Gregory had fallen head over heels in love with, was supposed to be.

Gregory and Abby were drifting across the stage toward each other, arms outstretched, hungry for their first embrace, when Laura flew out from the wings and separated them. Megan knew Julia's opening lines by heart: "There you are, my darling! Oh, Gregory, how wonderful you look—but surely you must be exhausted from your long journey." Head high, her brocade gown rustling, Laura inserted herself between the lovers, brushing Abby efficiently aside as if she were some sort of petty annoyance.

"Away with you, my sweet," she murmured, taking Gregory possessively by the arm. "I must have him all to myself now. William has drawn your bath, Gregory, and I've asked him to lay out fresh clothes for you, and then . . . and then . . ."

Julia paused, and Megan saw her stare at Gregory as if she'd never seen him before in her life. "And . . . and . . . then, my darling . . . my dearest . . . there's so much we have to talk about . . . so much to catch up on . . . all the news . . . all the news that . . ." Megan began to perspire even harder than when she'd wheeled up the ramp to the ferry.

Julia had forgotten her lines!

She was enough of a pro, however, that she was able

to muff her way through the remainder of the scene, using snatches of the few lines she could bring to mind, which unnerved poor Gregory (in real life, an accountant with a local tax firm) so badly that he had a hard time recalling his own.

Harris massaged his eyeballs vigorously with the heels of his palms. "Oh my God, just what I was afraid of," he groaned. "She's blowing it! What if this gets in the papers? What if some wire service picks it up? 'Famous Actress Bombs in Rare Charity Appearance.' It'll be the end of Julia; she'll never leave the apartment again till they carry her out on a stretcher with a sheet over her face!"

Megan leaned toward him, but felt a hand on her shoulder, restraining her. She turned, startled, to find Andrew crouched in the aisle beside her chair. A nervous twitch at the corner of his left eye made it seem as if he were winking.

"I'm sorry, but I wonder if you'd come backstage with me," he whispered, glancing at Harris. Megan rolled back to allow Harris to pass by.

"No, no," Andrew hissed, "it's *you* she wants!" Before Megan could say yea or nay, Andrew had turned her chair, then wheeled her briskly up the aisle toward the exit.

The remainder of act one was still in progress when they got backstage. In that scene, Megan remembered, Laura had left Gregory in the garden after he told her he needed a few moments to himself, and he lingered there, knowing that Abby would return. Andrew propelled

Megan between hangers of costumes, piles of stage furniture, and partly used cans of paint to a plain wood door that had been hung with a star made out of tinfoil. Whose hopeful touch had that been? Megan wondered.

Inside the small dressing room, Julia sat hunched before her makeup mirror, one clawlike hand gripping a half-empty glass of amber liquid. She was looking for courage again at the bottom of a glass, Megan realized.

She wheeled so close to Julia that her knees touched the actress's gown. Julia continued to stare into the mirror, her green eyes glazed with terror. "I can . . . scarcely remember . . . a thing!" she whispered dully. "My lines . . . I was so sure I had them etched into my brain . . . but the moment I saw Abby . . . they just flew like birds that'd been let out of a cage. There's no way I can go back out there and face—"

"Of course you can," Megan said matter-of-factly. The words shocked Julia so badly that she set her glass down with a clunk. "Sometimes there's no easy way to do something except just to do it."

Julia stared at her out of hopeless green eyes. "I'll stay in the wings," Megan offered. "If I'm there, maybe it'll help. That way, I can give you a prompt if you need it. That'll make it easier."

Julia moved her glass toward the back of her dressing table. "I'm not sure. . . ." She hesitated. "I must've panicked," she whispered. "You see, even during dress rehearsal, Abby didn't look so . . . you know, like she does tonight. Beside her, I look like a monstrous old crone—the wicked witch right out of *Snow White*."

"But in the play both you and Gregory *are* a lot older than Abby, remember?" Megan pointed out. "If you and Abby were the same age, there'd be no play, right? You're supposed to be older, Julia—and stronger and more determined and tougher—that's what *Call Back Yesterday* is all about—about a woman who's loved this dude for ages and ages and figured she was going to marry him someday and it'd be happily ever after. If the theater group had wanted a kitten for the part, they'd never have asked you to play Laura in the first place, right? What they wanted was someone who would"— Megan searched her mind desperately for the right phrase—"for someone who could break everybody's heart!" she finished.

"Break everybody's heart," Julia echoed softly. "Yes, I can do that, can't I?" She studied Megan with eyes that slowly became less glassy. "And you promise you'll be right there in the wings?"

"For sure," Megan said. "You couldn't beat me off with a stick."

Only twice, late in the second act and once at the beginning of the final scene, did Megan have to whisper a hoarse prompt to Julia. Then, in the last scene, she watched from the wings as Julia brooded alone on a stone bench in her ruined garden. It was autumn; leaves (silk ones, the program said, courtesy of the local novelty store in Aurora) were blown lightly around her feet by someone who held a hair dryer just offstage. The lovers had flown, leaving behind a message that they intended to be married and were on their way to Europe,

143

where Gregory would take up a post as conductor with the London Symphony and begin to live the life that Laura had always thought would be hers. Laura shook with sobs that soon had many in the audience at The Playhouse weeping noisily.

"Why did it have to be?" Laura breathed, her husky voice cracking with grief. "My life, my only love—gone now! All the years I waited, all the plans I made, lost, lost! I'll never be able to call back yesterday—" She rose from the bench and took three steps toward the audience. Her scarlet dress, together with her astonishing hair, made Julia look not like an aging woman but like a pillar of fire. Her face was ravaged by pain, yet beautiful in a way that Abby's perfect porcelain one had never been.

"Tomorrow—tomorrow I will begin again," Laura cried out. She held long, braceleted arms out to embrace the darkness beyond the proscenium. "And then I will begin again—and again." The cry came up from her heart, the declaration of a woman determined to go on living and loving.

There was a hushed stillness in the house, then waves of applause washed across the stage. Someone (had Andrew and Harris arranged it?) threw massive bouquets of white and yellow roses at Julia's feet. She bowed deeply, then blew kisses off the tips of her fingers into the darkness.

Megan blew her nose. She'd been crying and hadn't even known it. Julia had made Laura's grief so real that she'd felt it herself, even though the play had been the romantic kind she always teased Mom about. Laura's determination to live on after her lover's betrayal was like a knife in Megan's heart. "I'll begin again—and again!" Laura had vowed. But those were only words from a silly play, Megan told herself; even Julia had said so. Real life, whatever that was, wasn't like that. Or could it be?

**15**

The day dawned cloudy and cool. A brisk wind stirred the gray lake into a sulfurous froth, while the pines along the road that led down the hill to the ferry sighed restlessly, hinting at an early autumn.

Megan cinched the drawstring of the hood on her old navy sweat suit more snugly under her chin. She readjusted the belt she'd borrowed from Dad. She had threaded it around the back of her chair, and it now held her as securely in place as if she were in the bucket seat of a sports car. She'd grabbed the belt out of his closet at the last minute, when she realized she didn't want to risk the chance of tumbling onto the pavement if she and Harris got moving too fast.

Megan squinted uncertainly at the ominous sky, then back at the sullen yellow-green lake. "Listen, Harris, maybe we should postpone this till tomorrow," she suggested when he rolled up beside her. "By then, it might be warmer. Yuk; this kind of weather doesn't do major things for my competitive spirit, you know?''

She peered at him through the early-morning gloom, hoping he'd quickly agree with her and they could head back toward the cottages. It was an ideal day to stay indoors, to read, do quiet-type stuff. If he was hard to convince, she'd offer to make cookies.

Harris yawned and rubbed the sleep out of his eyes. They'd agreed three days ago to do this, but although she'd reminded him twice to set his alarm for six-thirty, he'd forgotten and Joey had had to be sent next door twenty minutes ago to pry him out of bed.

"Naw, we better stick to our plan," Harris advised, yawning again behind his hand. His ankle was almost completely healed, but he'd telephoned the mainland and told the rental supply company he'd need to keep his chair for at least three more weeks. What he didn't tell them was why, just in case they objected to having their equipment used the way he intended to use it.

"If we don't get started on this today like we said we would, M and M, it'll end up being another one of those things we talk about but never do because you get cold feet."

Megan raised her eyebrows. "Listen up, Harris. I've got an SCI, remember? Whether my feet are hot or cold never gets registered up here," she reminded him, tapping her forehead. Of course, what he mentioned about a change of heart was true: It really *would* be easier not to try, to convince herself that what they were planning to do was another dumb idea. To hide her awareness of that fact, Megan rubbed her hands briskly together and blew warm air on her red knuckles.

"Okay, coach," she grumbled, and they coasted slowly, their brakes lightly set, down the hill toward the deserted parking lot in front of the dock where the ferry loaded and unloaded three times a day. A half-dozen cars were huddled at the west end of the lot, like rain-soaked birds trying to shield themselves from the autumny weather. The rest of the lot was empty, its dark surface gleaming from last night's cold downpour. The first bunch of passengers had departed on the ferry half an hour ago; the next load wouldn't arrive till noon.

Megan studied the length of the lot through slitted eyes. "Wow. How long do you think it is?" she wondered out loud.

"At least a couple of blocks," Harris estimated. "Perfect for what we need. Just long enough for us to be able to work up a good head of steam."

But in the steely light of early morning what had seemed like a nifty idea on the night of Julia's victory in *Call Back Yesterday* now seemed questionable at best, crazy at worst.

Yet here I am, she realized, confronted with what I agreed to do. After that disaster at the Hideout, though, hadn't she promised herself she'd *never* try to pick up the pieces again? Wasn't this really just another whacked-out idea like the one to row out there had been?

Oh, for sure it had been fun to toss this racing idea back and forth with Harris while they were parked safely on the cottage porch on warm, sunny afternoons last week, but quite another to stare down the length of the deserted parking lot at seven o'clock on a cold August morning and imagine racing beside him to the end of it.

Megan shivered with regret, which Harris mistook for something else. "Hey, Megan, you won't feel so cold as soon as we start to practice," he consoled. Spray from the waves crashing against the dock dampened Megan's lips; she licked the moisture off with her tongue. "Well, then, I guess we better quit dinking around," she muttered without enthusiasm. She wheeled her chair quickly to the west end of the lot and turned to wait for him.

Across the angry waters the rising sun had slowly turned the misty air the color of ripe peaches. Overhead, gulls cried hungrily and swooped low through the fog, hoping the racers would offer treats.

"Just remember this is as new to me as it is to you," Harris cautioned, rolling up beside her, "so don't dump on me if I can't keep up."

"You're always making such a big deal out of what a wimp you are, Harris, but no matter what you say we both know you never lay flat on your back for three months like I did," Megan chided.

One of the terrible things about those days was there'd been no way she could escape herself, trussed up like a chicken in that Stryker frame. The worst part hadn't been the pain, the fear, the doctors, the nurses; the worst had been the knowledge that she couldn't get out of her own skin, was totally at the mercy of what other people decided to do with her and to her.

149

"Then when I finally was able to start therapy," Megan admitted softly, "I felt as if my whole body was made of mush. At first, I couldn't even roll myself into the shower, let alone do exercises. Someone had to push me in, then turn on the water for me." Now, those days seemed far enough away that she could talk about them safely.

"Sometimes I'd turn my face up and wonder if I could drown myself that way. It didn't work. I hardly had strength enough to wash my hair. Once I washed it, I didn't have pep enough left to rinse it. It was weeks before I could roll myself down the hall past the nurses' station. The therapists said there's nothing worse for a person's muscles than just lying in bed. No way, Harris, did you ever go through anything like that."

Harris nodded in silent agreement as they positioned themselves side by side at the edge of the parking lot. Megan gave her hood a final hitch. She checked to make sure her feet were planted firmly on her footrests and that the Velcro straps were fastened snugly across each instep. She loosened Dad's belt a notch so that she could lean forward more easily yet still be held securely against the back of her chair. She glanced at Harris.

"Ready?"

"Ready."

"One, two, three—go!" she cried.

Harris pushed off fast and quickly pulled into the lead. Megan remembered the trick she'd learned by accident on the path behind the cottages. *Bend low*, she reminded herself. *Stroke hard*.

Her chair leaped forward, and Megan felt Dad's belt bite into the flesh above her belly button. But even though she felt as if she were flying, Harris stayed three chair lengths in the lead. Her handrims burned against her palms, but no matter how fiercely she stroked she couldn't pass him before they reached the end of the parking lot.

"The winnah!" he yelled triumphantly, doing a wheelie on the slick pavement, and held a pair of clenched fists in the air. His glasses had fogged over with mist, and his cheeks were pink with effort. He was as childishly delighted with his victory as Joey would have been.

"Put it in your scrapbook, Harris, because I'll run right over you next time!" Megan warned. She wouldn't let him get the jump on her again; she'd be the one to pull out fast this time, would grab the lead, then hang on to it for dear life. An old, familiar determination seized her, as if it'd been standing right behind her, a phantom waiting to catch up with her, the sort of will-power that once had made it easy for her to put points on the board in games against the Rockettes.

"You count this time," she said, dropping so low over her knees that she could feel her collarbone press against her kneecaps. When Harris yelled "Go!", she shot forward before he had a chance to stroke his wheels a quarter of a turn.

Headed away from the rising sun, their twin shadows were cast faintly before them on the wet, gleaming parking lot. Watching those fleeing shadows, Megan knew suddenly who she was trying to outrun. *Me*, she realized; it's the old me I'm competing against, against the person I was a year ago. Not Harris, not anyone I might meet three weeks from now at the HandiFair, only me. She stroked her handrims harder, harder, until her hands were scorched and the effort to outrun Harris had built a fire in her chest, making her exhale in great, smoky wheezes.

She didn't permit herself the luxury of a backward glance to see if Harris was gaining. She slowed only when she got within twenty yards of the parked cars. When she finally turned it was to discover he was still several chair lengths in the rear. This time it was her turn to raise a pair of fists in the air.

"Guaranteed not to melt in your hand!" She laughed.

Harris braked his chair squarely in front of her. "Well, what do you know? A first," he remarked softly.

"You kidding?" Megan retorted with a cocky toss of her head. "I've won other races. Matter of fact, I placed first in the three-hundred-yard dash when I was in eighth grade." Maybe when she got home she'd ask Mom to bring down that framed picture from her old room, the one Dad had had enlarged from the newspaper clipping. Maybe it was still a part of her life after all, a part she didn't have to leave hanging in an empty room under the eaves close to the stars.

"That's not what I meant."

"What then?"

"You laughed. I mean *really* laughed. An up-from-the-gut laugh. I was beginning to think you'd taken a religious vow against mirth.'' Harris smiled himself. ''Know something, Megan? You're sort of lit up now, like there's a little candle right behind your eyes that's shining out at me.''

Megan glanced away quickly. Hadn't Joey said practically the same thing, that he liked it best when she was happy? She pressed her burning fingers to her mouth. Her lips were still curled in a smile, her whole face felt softer. Megan closed her eyes and tipped her face up to the morning sun, letting its rays warm her mist-dampened cheeks. Once again, she had that queer, waking-up-from-a-long-nap feeling, as if she were a princess in a fairy tale, one who'd been put to sleep by a wicked witch's curse.

But you're not a princess, Megan reminded herself. After the accident maybe the curse was one you laid on yourself.

''So you want to race one more time?'' she invited, eyes still closed. She opened her lids just enough to sneak a peek at Harris through a raggedy fringe of wet lashes. ''To see if I can beat you again?'' she taunted slyly.

When Harris got the jump at the starting line, Megan was confident she could catch him. She quickly realized she was mistaken; Harris pumped hard to stay in the lead, wouldn't give her an inch. Her eagerness of moments before turned briefly to resentment that boiled sourly in her chest, until it dawned on her what he was doing.

*He cares enough not to make this easy for me*, Megan

153

realized. *He's not going to give me this race—or any other race—just to make me feel good in the short term. He's thinking about the long term, about how nothing good will happen if he goes soft on me.*

Sweat dampened her armpits and the back of her neck, soaked the waistband of her old blue sweat pants. Harris edged her out by a single chair length and was panting hard himself when they halted at the edge of the parking lot.

Megan loosened her hood, the chill of half an hour ago forgotten. She filled her lungs with damp lake air, while Harris draped himself like a soggy towel over the arm of his chair, exhausted.

"Listen, if we keep this up for three more weeks, I bet you could be a real contender," he gasped.

"Wait . . . a . . . minute, Harris," she cautioned, panting, too. "I never said for sure that I'd enter the HandiFair race. You just took it for granted. Anyway, this isn't one of Julia's movies. You know, the kind where the plucky heroine goes sailing across the finish line, a champion, while her family bursts into tears and violins swell in the background and specators yell 'We always knew you could do it!' Face it, Harris, people who compete in a race like the HandiFair have been practicing for months. No way am I going to get good enough to win in three weeks."

The wind nibbled at her short, pale bangs and cooled the nape of her neck. But if she *did* decide to enter the HandiFair—and she hadn't, not yet—what would it be like? Megan asked herself. How would it feel to get together with a bunch of people who were just like she was, everyone in wheelchairs, everyone with a story to tell about how they'd gotten there?

Megan wasn't sure she was ready for what it might mean.

It would finally be an admission that nothing would ever be like it used to be, right?

Because isn't that what had always been her secret hope, that it would? That she'd wake up some morning and find out it had all been a bad dream, that she was the same old Megan, that there'd never been a Dex Cooper, no motorcycle, no accident?

Megan squinted into the distance, where, floating on the water that was now the color of warm peach sauce, the Hideout was alternately hidden and revealed through shimmering curtains of mist. She patted the arms of her chair.

"Know something, Harris?"

"Not much."

"Before summer's over I'd like to go back."

"Back where?"

"Out there."

"Out there?"

"Yeah. Back to the Hideout."

Harris followed her glance across the water. "We could do it right this time," Megan explained. "We'd tell everybody where we were going so nobody'd have to worry about us."

"We could take Joey," Harris suggested, pleased.

"Maybe we could."

"Rollie, too."

"Yeah, Rollie'd love it out there."

"It'd be sort of like . . . like we were a family." Harris's voice was soft, happy.

Until this moment, it had never occurred to Megan that she had anything to give him. She couldn't be a girlfriend, for sure not until she found out a few more things about herself. But maybe she could give him something he'd never had before. A little brother. A dog. An island called the Hideout.

"Yeah, Harris," she agreed softly, "like we were a family. Sort of like we were—" Megan hesitated. The image that bloomed in her head surprised her. She smiled. "Sort of like we were the Swiss Family Robinson and we were going off to settle in a wild and dangerous land where we might have to make do and go without."

# 16

"Mail call!" Dad yelled when he hopped out of the car. But there was more than mail in the two bags he carried up the ramp into the cottage. He'd also brought a watermelon, two cartons of ruby-red strawberries as big as hen's eggs, and a fragrant batch of still-warm cabbage rolls that Mrs. Adler had sent up for supper.

"Hey, buddy, I've got some postcards for you," he called to Joey through the screen door. "Guess everyone on the block misses you like crazy."

Mom unloaded the sack and began to put things in the fridge. "I think there's a card in there for you, too, sweetie," Dad told her, "and unless I miss my guess it's from Paris." He rolled his eyes. "You got a boyfriend I don't know about? They say a husband is always the last to know."

"Oh, goody!" Mom squealed. "Sallie didn't forget me after all." She immediately quit what she was doing and sat down with a big smile to read what Mrs. Chambliss had written.

"Ummm . . . and there's even something for you, Megan," Dad said, dropping an envelope in the middle of the kitchen table, then taking over Mom's job of putting the groceries away.

Surprised, Megan glanced up from making a list of stuff she wanted to take to the Hideout. It never occurred to her to ask if there was anything for her too. She'd succeeded in putting everyone at home so thoroughly out of her mind that she assumed they'd done the same with her. It'd be kind of neat, though, if Bev had decided to write. Megan picked up the letter that lay facedown next to the sugar bowl. It was in a business-style envelope; it couldn't be from Bev, who loved stationery with cuddly animals or fat angels printed on it.

Megan turned the envelope over. It was addressed to Megen Murphy. She frowned; Megen? Excuse me! Whoever had taken the time to write didn't even know how to spell her name.

She peered at the address in the upper left corner. The handwriting was unfamiliar, the large letters clumsily printed and childish. Gee, maybe it was meant for Joey, not for her at all. She checked the postmark.

San Diego, California.

Oh.

There was only one person she knew who lived in California.

Suddenly, Megan's heart felt funny, bruised and lumpy in her chest. She rolled herself into her room on the porch and laid the letter on the medicine cart. She reached for the cranberry juice and took a big swig.

Maybe it'd be better not to open it. She did, finally, but didn't unfold the letter right away.

Did she really want to read anything Dex might have to say? she wondered, turning to stare across the water at the Hideout. I don't have to, she reminded herself. I can quit any time it starts to hurt too much. Then she unfolded the piece of paper. When she began to read, it seemed as if the words floated off the page one at a time, rose to meet her glance, and asked permission to enter her head and her heart.


Dear Megen:

Maybe you won't believe this, but I've thought about you practically every day since the accident. You were the one who got hurt real bad, not me, which makes people think the accident happened only to you. And mostly that's true, because you're the one who won't ever walk again.

But you want to know something, Megen? In a way it happened to me too.

At the hospital I went by your room once. 240A, right? See, I still remember. Maybe you didn't even know I was on the same floor you were, but I was, for almost two weeks. Know why I never came in to see you, even though I really wanted to? Because I couldn't think of the right thing to say, that's why. I mean, what do you say to somebody after you've wrecked their life, huh?

Soon as I got back to school, all anybody could talk about was how you'd be in a wheelchair for always. That you'd never play basketball again. I think about that every day, Megen, because that's where I first saw you, in that big game you played against the Rockettes. I try to imagine what it'd be like if it was me instead of you that had gotten busted up. I guess I'd be pretty mad at the person who'd done it to me, so I know how you must feel about me.

So what I wanted to tell you, Megen, is I'm sorry. Sorry I didn't know about that new gravel. Sorry I was going too fast. I'll be sorry the rest of my life. Well, Megen, I just wanted you to know. Good-bye. And good luck, too.

Your friend,
Dexter A. Cooper

Your friend, Dexter A. Cooper. Until this moment, she'd never wondered if he had a middle name. Maybe it was Arthur. Or Anthony. Megan let the letter lie in her lap.

Did what he'd written change anything? For sure it didn't mean she'd suddenly leap out of her chair to the sound of swelling violins and walk again as if nothing had happened. No. The letter didn't mean that. So it was probably true that words couldn't make a difference.

Except that they did.

Megan fingered the sharp edge of the folded paper. For starters, it meant that one day out there in San Diego, California, Dexter A. Cooper had hunted through his dad's house for a piece of paper. If he had a stepmother, he probably had to ask her for an envelope. He'd hustled up a stamp somewhere. Then he sat down to write.

Finally, he'd sealed it and dropped it in the mail, maybe on his way to hang out with somebody. For so many months she'd imagined that it didn't matter to him, that he'd gone back to his West Coast life with a shrug. But he'd cared enough to write *I'll be sorry the rest of my life*.

"Who was your letter from, Meggie?" Mom called from the kitchen.

Outside, Megan could hear Dad and Joey talking to Harris down on the beach. "No one special. Just somebody I used to know at Hudson," she called back evasively. Right now, she wanted to savor how queerly sweet and tender her heart felt, as if it were new and had started to beat for the first time.


When the boat was finally loaded, Dad leaned over the dock and lowered Rollie into it by his front legs. Harris pushed off, and Joey held Rollie while Megan took up the oars.

"Be careful," Mom called.

"Don't let it get too late before you start back," Dad urged.

"Remember to take some pictures," Andrew suggested.

"Have a wonderful time, you three! Of course I know I never have to worry about you, Harris!" Julia cried.

"But there's four of us, Mrs. St. John," Joey yelled back through a megaphone made of his palms. "You forgot to count Rollie!"

Joey insisted on having a turn at rowing toward the

Hideout. "No fair for you to have all the fun, Megan," he complained.

"All right already," she said, giving up the oars to him and taking charge of Rollie, who seemed to want to leap into the water and swim all the way to the Hideout. It was warm, with only a vague hint of autumn in the air, not like it had been a few days ago at the parking lot.

"Save a turn for me," Harris reminded Joey. "I gotta stay in shape, you know, if I'm gonna keep up with this sister of yours."

Joey shrugged. "If a person's gotta have a sister, she's not too bad."

"Gee, don't squander any compliments on me or I might get a swelled head," Megan grumbled, smiling.

When they finally reached the Hideout, Joey gave Harris strict instructions about how far to pull the *Dolly* onto the beach. "I don't want to get stranded out here like you dopes almost did," he observed sternly.

"Don't worry, kid, I only make the same mistake once. Of course I keep making new ones—"

Joey shot Harris a startled glance. "Just kidding, Joey," Harris murmured. "Don't clutch up."

"What'd we bring to eat?" Joey wanted to know, relieved. "I'm hungry already."

"We've got lots of stuff. Marshmallows, even, if we decide to stay late."

"Remember what Dad said," Joey reminded her.

"It's okay, Joey," Harris broke in. "I told your dad we'd probably have a campfire. There'll be a moon out tonight so rowing back to the island will be a cinch."

162

"We can even tell ghost stories!" Joey exclaimed. "Me and Megan used to do it all the time."

Joey and Harris sat cross-legged on the blanket while Megan rested her back against *Dolly* and they ate fried chicken, watermelon, and dozens of strawberries. Julia sent brownies along too, and to Megan's amazement they were almost as good as Mom's.

"So now me and Harris are gonna go into the woods and get stuff for our fire tonight," Joey announced when they'd finished eating. "You be okay while we're gone, Megan?"

"For sure," she told them, waving them away. Actually, she was glad they had something to do. Because there was something she wanted to do. And she wanted to do it here, alone, on the beach at the Hideout. As soon as they disappeared into the woods, she took paper and a pen out of the lunch bag, used the box that Julia had packed brownies in as a desk, and began to write.

Dear Dexter:

I got your letter. Thanks for writing it. I'm sitting on the beach at one of my favorite places. For a long time I thought I'd never be able to come here ever again, but maybe even when you're in a wheelchair you can still decide to do whatever you want to do.

Yes, I knew you were on the same floor I was. I knew you came by my room once, too. I always wondered why you didn't come in. I guess I didn't stop to think about how the accident was for you. I was so sure it had happened only to me.

Maybe it'll make you feel better to know what I'm going to do two weeks from now. I'm going to enter a wheelchair race. A friend of mine named Harris got me the entry forms, and he's been helping me train for it.

For a long time I didn't think I ever wanted to see you again, but if you ever come back to Hudson to visit your mom, why don't you come by? Maybe it'd make both of us feel better if we could talk about what happened.

But that's over. We've both got to get used to how our lives are now. Thanks again for writing to me, Dexter. Good luck to you too.

Your friend,
Megan (the Magnificent)

Megan folded the letter just as Harris and Joey came back carrying enough wood for a whole week's worth of campfires. She smiled up at them. Funny; she'd never realized letting go would feel so good.

Across the lake, the orange lights of the two cottages were reflected in the smooth, black water, and in the moonlight a solitary rowboat returning from a day of fishing could be seen moving toward the distant shore. Joey, full of marshmallows, had curled himself up in a blanket, Rollie at his side, dozing too. Megan and Harris sat close, staring into the fire.

"You feel like you'll be ready to race next week?" he asked.

"Ready as I'll ever be," Megan said, and sighed. "Not that I expect even to place. I hear there's a girl from Spencer, Iowa, who's entered who's really a sharpie. She won last year."

"Ever find out how she ended up in a wheelchair?"

"Birth injury, I think," Megan said, remembering the brief bio she'd read in the material that came with confirmation of her entry forms. There were so many ways a person could end up being someone other than who they thought they ought to be.

Harris fished in his pocket, then held out his open palm. Megan looked down to see several small stones lying there. "I think I'll make some wishes," he said. He lobbed a pebble out into the lake, where it made a sound as soft as a kiss.

"What'd you wish?" Megan asked.

"That Julia and Andrew and I could come back here next year."

"The Chamblisses might rent the cottage again," Megan warned.

"Then maybe we can find another one close by."

"Give me a stone too," Megan asked. She plucked one out of his palm and pitched it into the black water.

"You going to tell me your wish?" Harris wondered.

"I wished yours would come true."

Harris reached across the blanket and closed his hand over hers. His fingers were warm, not cold and quivery as they'd been the day they'd been stranded here.

"One of them already did," he said. There was a smile in his voice. "The one about Julia. She called home yesterday and got the messages off her answering machine. There's a producer looking for an older actress to play somebody's grandmother. Julia says she'll do it."

"*Grand*mother?" In the dark, Megan smiled. Wow; Julia was really getting into real life.

165

"Grandma?" Joey echoed sleepily. "Did somebody say our grandma was—"

"Shush, Joey," Megan whispered. "Go back to sleep."

Harris squeezed her hand. "Look at Joey," he whispered. "He's zonked. I'll probably have to load him in the boat just like I load you." He smiled. His eyes, mild and happy behind his glasses, were warm in the firelight. He laced his fingers with hers and together they gazed into the dying fire.

"Know something, Harris?" Megan asked.

"Not much," he admitted.

"As summers go, maybe this was a pretty good one after all," she said, and squeezed his fingers back.